BARNEY
HITS THE TRAIL

ILLUSTRATED BY FRED MACHETANZ

SARA AND FRED
MACHETANZ

BARNEY

HITS THE TRAIL

THE JUNIOR LITERARY GUILD AND
CHARLES SCRIBNER'S SONS • NEW YORK

TO
MOM

CONTENTS

BARNEY
HITS THE TRAIL

1

BARNEY'S BIRTHDAY PRESENT

Barney came bursting through the front door.

"Dinner ready?" he called. He knew there would be something special because today was his birthday.

Mother popped her head out of the kitchen.

"Don't you come in the kitchen now, Barney, you stay away from here till I call."

Barney grinned. So she *was* cooking something special.

"All right," he agreed, then he sat down on the couch and sniffed the air to try and guess what was cooking.

The kitchen door opened just a crack and Barney's little sister, Fran, peered out. "I know a secret, I know a secret! I'll give you three guesses—"

1

"Fran," Mother came to the door and pulled her back into the kitchen, "you come back in here and help me!"

Barney laughed. Fran never could keep a secret.

Just then, the front door opened and Dad came in carrying a big package.

"Hello, Dad!"

"Hello, Son. How did it feel being eleven years old today?"

"Not much different," and it really didn't feel much different. "What do you have there, Dad?" Barney asked pointing to the package his Dad was holding.

"Never you mind, Son," and Dad disappeared into the kitchen.

"Now what in the world could be in that package?" Barney wondered.

Mother and Dad had given him their birthday present that morning. It was a lifetime fountain pen with his name engraved on the side. Uncle Bill and Aunt Helen had sent a wallet. Fran had given him the new leather belt he was wearing, so it couldn't very well be another birthday present. Just the same he wondered what might be in the package.

He could hear voices in the kitchen. They were talking a lot about something, but he couldn't make out

what they were saying. After what seemed like a long time, Mother called that dinner was ready.

In one leap Barney was off the couch and across the room. As he opened the kitchen door, he could smell homemade rolls baking and hear chicken sizzling in a skillet. In the center of the table was a big white cake with a circle of eleven candles, and one to grow on in the middle. But the thing that caught his eye was a big package in the place where his plate should have been.

Just then, the whole family—Mother, Dad and Fran—started singing Happy Birthday. Mother and Fran kissed him, although he didn't like that much. Barney laughingly pulled away and rushed over to the table.

"Unalakleet, Alaska!" he shouted, looking at the postmark. "This must be from Uncle Charlie!" Barney's Uncle Charlie ran a Trading Post in an Eskimo village.

Fran was skipping around the table clapping her hands, "Open it, Barney, open it!"

Barney didn't need urging. He tore off the wrapping and pulled back the flaps of the cardboard carton. In it were some bundles done up in brown paper. The first package he took out felt squnchy. Excitedly, he took off the paper and opened it.

"Why, it's a pair of fur boots!"

"Well, so it is!" Dad came closer for a good look.

"Put them on, Barney and see if they fit," Mother suggested.

Barney quickly took off his shoes to try on the boots. They were very light and soft. When he pulled the first one on, he felt something prick his foot. It was a card. On it in Uncle Charlie's handwriting were the words:

"These are Eskimo boots. They are called *mukluks* and you will wear them most of the time."

Barney let out a whoop. "Imagine me wearing those to deliver papers!"

Mother smiled, "See what else is in the box," she urged.

Before she could finish, Barney had already taken out a very large bundle.

"Now, what do you suppose this can be?" he asked, but didn't wait for anyone to guess before he unwrapped it and held up a fur slipover coat.

"Why it's an Eskimo parka!" Mother said.

Barney could hardly wait to slip the parka over his head. It was light and warm and had a leathery smell. It reached a little below his knees and was just the right size. He looked for a card but couldn't find one.

Then Fran saw a white paper corner sticking out of the cuff. It was the card, and it read:

> "This parka is made of reindeer fur. The fur around the hood is wolf, to protect your face when the temperature is fifty degrees below."

Barney couldn't believe it. All these fine fur clothes were really his!

"Let me try it on, Barney," Fran begged, "please let me try on your parka?"

"Go ahead," Barney agreed, "but it'll be too big for you."

He held up the parka while Fran slid in.

"Oh, I can't see anything, I can't breathe!" she cried in a faraway voice.

Mother and Dad were looking at Fran and laughing so hard, they could scarcely see. Barney stepped back for a look. All he could see was the back of Fran's head in the opening of the parka hood.

"You're wearing it backwards, Franny," Barney explained, as he helped her take it off. When Fran saw all the others laughing, she laughed too.

Dad was first to catch his breath.

"I guess your arithmetic teacher could wear your parka the way Fran did, Barney."

"What do you mean, Dad?"

"Well, I've heard you say she has eyes in the back of her head," Dad said, and they all laughed again.

There was one more package. Barney eagerly ripped it open and found two oblong pieces of dark grey fur.

Dad picked up one of them.

"It's fur mitts, Barney, and they look large enough for me," he said, pulling one on.

Barney took a card out of the thumb of the other mitt he was trying for size.

"No, they're for me. Just made big enough to go over wool gloves. See what Uncle Charlie has written."

"These mitts of wolf are made to go over your regular wool gloves when driving the dogs in cold weather."

Dad put the card down on the table.

"Then I won't get a chance to wear them after all," he joked, and handed the grey fur mitt back to Barney. "I guess they're for you right enough. But when. . . ."

"That's just what I was wondering," Barney said as he took the mitt. "When *can* I wear them? From what Uncle Charlie says, all of these clothes are to be worn in real cold weather out on the trail with the dogs.

Doesn't Uncle Charlie know we don't drive dog teams down here?"

Dad smiled. "I guess he does realize you wouldn't have much use for this fur outfit down here, Barney," then he drew a white envelope out of his pocket.

"Here, he sent this to you, too."

Barney opened the envelope and found three tickets. One was a train ticket from Porterville to Minneapolis, another was an airline ticket from Minneapolis to Anchorage, Alaska, and the third an airline ticket from Anchorage, Alaska, to Unalakleet, the Eskimo village where Uncle Charlie lived.

Barney was flabbergasted. He stared and stared at the tickets. His heart began to pound. Could it possibly mean that Uncle Charlie was sending him tickets to come to Unalakleet? He looked at Dad. Dad was smiling and nodding.

"Uncle Charlie wants you to come and live with him this winter. He's lonely and he wants some one to help him run his Trading Post."

Barney opened his mouth to say something but no words came. He was so surprised he couldn't speak.

Fran was watching him with her eyes dancing.

"I told you I knew a secret. You didn't think I

could keep a secret all to myself, did you . . ."

Mother broke in, "You can go to school with the Eskimos, Barney. Uncle Charlie says there is a good school in Unalakleet."

Go to school with the Eskimos!

Barney leaned forward so far on his chair, he almost fell off.

"When do I go?" he asked and held his breath for the answer.

"Let's see now," Dad looked at the calendar and figured.

"Today is Wednesday. You can finish your paper route Friday. I've already talked to your principal at school and he tells me it will be possible for you to transfer at the end of the week. I'd say you can take the train out of here Friday night and the plane from Minneapolis for Alaska Saturday morning. According to Uncle Charlie, you'll be in Unalakleet by Sunday. That means you won't lose a single day of school."

"Do you mean to say I will be with Uncle Charlie *all* winter?"

"If you want to, Barney. Mother and I think it'll be fine for you."

"Do I want to? Do I want to?" Barney was almost

shouting. He couldn't sit down any longer. He jumped up and started walking back and forth.

"Why, I can wear my new fur clothes—I can drive a dog team out on trail, I can—"

"Oh, Barney, bring me some fur boots and a parka for my doll when you come back?" Fran ran to her brother and threw her arms around him. "I want some Eskimo clothes for my doll. Please, please bring me some."

"Okay, Franny," Barney promised before he quite realized what he was saying. "I'll bring your doll an Eskimo outfit." Then, suddenly it came to him that he was making the trip *alone*, that he was leaving his Mother and Dad behind. There was a queer tight feeling in his throat. He swallowed hard and said: "What shall I bring you, Mom?"

"You just bring yourself back, Barney. That will be plenty for me." Mother smiled at him and the tight feeling came back into his throat.

"That's easy," he said. "How about you, Dad, what do you want me to bring you from Alaska?"

Dad put on the very solemn face which he always used when he and Barney were joking.

"Well, I'll tell you what, Son. You might look

around up there and discover a gold mine for me, unless you'll be too busy doing other things."

"A gold mine! Do you mean there's gold where I'm going?"

"That's right," Dad wasn't joking any longer. "That's why your Uncle Charlie went up there in the first place—to look for gold. He never found any but maybe you'll have better luck."

Barney began to get excited all over again.

"Jeepers! I'm sure going to look, Dad, and—"

Mother interrupted. "If you two men can stop dreaming of discovering gold long enough to eat Barney's birthday dinner, I think we'll sit down. After all, we have a lot to do in the next two days if we're going to get Barney off to Alaska."

Two days! Only tomorrow and the next day and then Barney would be off to Alaska to live with Uncle Charlie and drive a dog team and look for gold.

2

UNALAKLEET

Barney fastened the leather seat belt over his hips without taking his eyes from the plane window.

It seemed only a few hours instead of two nights and a day since he had said good-bye to the family at Porterville. And now the plane was coming into Unalakleet! Far below, Barney could make out some dark blotches on the beach beside the Bering Sea. Somewhere down there was Uncle Charlie, and Eskimos and sled dogs and who could tell—maybe gold!

The red light at the front of the plane flashed on, warning passengers of a landing.

The plane made a steep bank and began to lose altitude. Barney felt as if his stomach was coming up in his throat but he was used to that after twenty hours of flying. There was a slight bump, another and another, then the plane taxied smoothly over the air field.

Barney undid his seat belt and grabbing up his box of fur clothes raced to the open door at the back of the plane.

The first thing he saw was a noisy crowd of Eskimos. They were all smiling, waving and chattering. Some wore fur parkas, others wore parkas of bright red, blue and green cloth. Sled dog puppies romped in and out of the crowd, barking excitedly.

Barney looked beyond the friendly crowd for a glimpse of his new home. Half a mile away was the log-cabin village of Unalakleet. All around the land was flat. To his right was the dark green Bering Sea and in the distance to the left were some hills and mountains. Nowhere could Barney see a single tree.

Just then, a large man, much taller than the Eskimos, stepped forward.

"Hello, Barney, welcome to Unalakleet!"

"Hello, Uncle Charlie!" Barney shouted and broke into a big grin.

Uncle Charlie turned to the crowd.

"This is my nephew from the States. His name is Barney."

The Eskimos grinned and nodded. Barney grinned and nodded back to them.

"And now," Uncle Charlie turned back to Barney, "I expect you'd like to see your new home."

"You bet I would! I can't wait."

Uncle Charlie took Barney's bags and handed them to three Eskimo boys. They raced ahead, chased by yelping sled pups and shouting children.

A fourth boy just about Barney's age came up.

"Let me help you with your box," he offered.

Barney hesitated. This was the box full of the precious fur clothes Uncle Charlie had sent.

"Well—" Barney said uncertainly.

"I'll be careful," the boy assured him smiling.

"Okay," Barney agreed and handed him the fur clothes.

"Koo-yah-nah," the boy said.

"That means 'thank you' in Eskimo," Uncle Charlie explained. "This is Anagik, Barney, you'll probably be seeing a lot of each other. He's in your grade at school."

"Welcome to Unalakleet," Anagik said.

"Koo-yah-nah," Barney replied and they both laughed. Uncle Charlie clapped Barney on the shoulder.

"You're going to get along fine, I can see that. Now let's get going."

The rest of the Eskimos, still laughing and talking, formed in a noisy parade behind Barney, Uncle Charlie and Anagik. They all started down a path toward the village.

"This is the main street of Unalakleet," Uncle Charlie told Barney.

"It called Charles Traeger Street," one of the Eskimo girls behind them said and burst into giggles.

"That's a fact," agreed Uncle Charlie. "Named for me!"

Barney gazed at the sandy path. If Uncle Charlie hadn't told him, he would never have believed this was a main street anywhere. He looked ahead toward the village and blinked his eyes to make sure he wasn't imagining things. A lot of the little log cabins were perched on poles above the ground.

"Look, Uncle Charlie, what's that little house up in the air?" Barney pointed to the one nearest him.

"Oh, that's a cache where Eskimos store their food

and furs. It's raised off the ground so animals can't get in."

Barney hardly waited for the answer before he had another question ready.

"What is the windmill for beside that cabin?" There were many windmills, some beside the cabins, some on cabin roofs.

"To make electricity for radios," Uncle Charlie explained. "Most of the Eskimos have radios and do you know what?"

"What?"

"Their favorite singer is Gene Autry."

"No fooling!"

They walked on a little way and Barney thought of something else.

"I'd always heard Eskimos lived in igloos."

"They do. So do you. Igloo is the Eskimo word for house."

Barney was certainly surprised. In that case his Dad and Mother and Fran lived in an igloo.

Now he saw still another kind of log cabin. It had no windows and was set low on the ground.

"Uncle Charlie, there aren't any windows in that house. Do people live there?"

Uncle Charlie laughed and shook his head.

"No, people don't live there. That's a dog barn where sled dogs are kept in very cold weather. Most of the dogs in the village stay out in all kinds of weather, though. Their coats are so thick they don't mind."

Barney heard more giggling behind him. He decided not to ask any further questions until he and Uncle Charlie were alone.

Beside each cabin Barney saw sled dogs chained to posts. They were beautiful, big, strong animals. Barney looked at them closely, trying to decide which ones he would pick for *his* team. The sled dogs set up a great howling as the crowd moved through the village.

"They're glad you've come," Anagik said to Barney and everyone laughed.

"They're really welcoming you to Unalakleet and your future home. Over there is the Trading Post," Uncle Charlie pointed to a large two-story building at the left. It was made of logs, covered with sheet-iron painted green. It looked like a warehouse of some sort.

At the door, Barney turned to his new Eskimo friends and invited them to come and see him. He took his fur clothes from Anagik and shook hands.

"Be seeing you," Anagik said.

"I hope so," Barney answered. He knew he and Anagik were going to be friends. Then he and Uncle Charlie went inside.

The room they came into was a large one with counters on each side and a big iron stove in the center. Barney could see shelves behind the counters loaded with all kinds of goods. Traps and furs hung down from the ceiling over the counters. The room smelled of furs and wood fires. Barney liked it.

"I have two Eskimo clerks to help me. You'll meet them when the Post opens tomorrow," Uncle Charlie said as they walked to the rear of the store. "This is the Unalakleet Post Office," he went on.

The Post Office!

Barney gaped at the rows of letter boxes in a back corner.

"Why I never thought of Eskimos getting mail!"

"No, I suppose you didn't. It comes in every Friday by plane."

"Then I won't have any trouble sending Christmas presents home, will I?"

"No, nor in receiving them either," Uncle Charlie

teased. "Now let's go upstairs and see your new home."

At the head of the steps was a big kitchen. A little old Eskimo man with a bald head and bright black eyes was standing before the stove stirring a pan full of something that smelled delicious.

"Barney, this is Velik, one of the best cooks on the west coast of Alaska."

"How do, how do," Velik made a half bow at Barney. "Glad you here."

"I'm glad to be here."

Uncle Charlie broke in, "I guess you'd like to wash up after your trip, wouldn't you, Barney?"

"Yes, I would."

Uncle Charlie walked over to two big barrels sitting on a low shelf at the end of the room. He turned a spigot at the bottom of one of them and filled a pan of water.

"In summer we get water out of the Unalakleet River. It is carried up here in buckets and emptied into these hogsheads. After freeze-up we have to chop ice out of the river and fill our barrels with that. Water is precious up here. In fact," his eyes twinkled, "if you won't write home about it, you'll only have to take one bath a week."

After they had washed, Uncle Charlie took Barney into a room at the right of the stairs.

"This is where you'll bunk."

There was a bed, a chest of drawers, an oil stove and two windows with double panes of glass.

"To keep out the cold," Uncle Charlie told him. "When winter comes, the wind blows so hard, snow drifts as high as these windows."

Barney looked down the twenty feet to the ground. It was hard to believe.

"You'd better unpack now. I'll be in the front room if you want me," Uncle Charlie said and left him.

Barney hurried with his unpacking. That walk from the plane in the crisp Alaskan air had given him an appetite. The sooner he unpacked, the sooner they could eat. He was just putting away his last pair of socks when he heard a strange, mournful sound. Moans and howls seemed to fill the air and spread through the village. Barney had never heard such a scary sound. Suddenly, he decided he didn't want to be alone. He ran out of the room.

"Wh-what's that noise, Uncle Charlie?"

Uncle Charlie looked at Barney's scared face and laughed.

"You don't need to worry, Barney. Those sounds don't come from wolves. It's the sled dogs howling. You'll hear that sound for the rest of your stay at Unalakleet."

"It sure sounded weird."

"Yes, there's no other sound like the moan of sled dogs."

Knowing what the noise was made Barney feel better. He looked around the front room. It was very large, so large, that he counted thirteen windows on three sides of it. There were half a dozen army cots against the walls. Uncle Charlie explained these were for travelers who passed through the village. There were shelves of books, comfortable furniture, a big wood stove, a radio and a phonograph.

"It's super," Barney said. "I didn't think I'd be so comfortable. How'd you get all this stuff up here?"

"Why, by ship, of course," Uncle Charlie answered, "our food comes by ship, too, during the summer. We have to order enough to last all winter because, after freeze-up, no ships come in till the ice goes out next spring. That's why we're so anxious for another boat to come in. Otherwise we'll run short of supplies."

"When do you expect the boat?"

"Any day now but it had better hurry. Frost has already turned the tundra grass brown. Freeze-up's getting near."

There was a knock at the head of the stairs.

"Come in!" Uncle Charlie called.

A white haired Eskimo walked into the front room.

"Hello, Nipchuk, I'm glad you came by. I want you to meet my nephew, Barney."

Nipchuk grinned and handed Barney a bundle.

"Something for the newcomer," he said in English.

"Go ahead and open it, Barney," Uncle Charlie urged.

Barney laid the bundle on a table and pushed the paper back. He thought he'd had his share of surprises for one day but this was another one. His present turned out to be, of all things, a fine, fat duck the Eskimo had shot that afternoon! Nipchuk told how he'd seen a flock of ducks flying south and brought down two with one shot.

"That was certainly nice of you to bring me one of your two ducks, Nipchuk. Koo-yah-nah."

Now it was Nipchuk's turn to be surprised.

"Him speak Eskimo?" he asked Uncle Charlie in amazement.

"A little," Uncle Charlie said and winked at Barney. "That duck will make mighty fine eating tonight," he added.

Nipchuk grinned widely at both of them, then backed to the door and with a wave and a nod, left.

"Well, you certainly set him back," Uncle Charlie laughed again, "but it was swell of him to bring the duck. There's no better meat than wild duck. I guess you and I'll have to clean it, since Velik's busy."

After the duck had been scalded and the feathers pulled out, Barney helped Uncle Charlie do the cleaning.

"Wait a minute there, you almost threw away the gizzard!"

"Gee, I did, didn't I?"

Barney picked up the gizzard and slit it down the middle as he had seen his mother do when fixing Sunday chicken. When he emptied the grit, he noticed some tiny dull yellow pebbles.

"Look here, Uncle Charlie, this duck's been eating something yellow."

"What's that? Let's see." Uncle Charlie took up the gizzard and looked.

"Great Christopher! *Gold*!"

"Gold!" Barney echoed not believing his ears.

"Yes, *gold*. Velik, Velik, look what Barney's found!"

Velik rushed over to the table.

"Ah-ree-gah! Gold!"

"It's gold, Barney, gold nuggets! This duck has been where there's gold."

"Gold!" Barney gasped and took another look at the particles. "You mean those yellow pebbles are real gold?"

"That's what they are," Uncle Charlie said.

Then Dad was right! There *was* gold in this country.

Velik was rubbing his hands together and hopping from one foot to the other. Barney felt as if he would explode from excitement. Uncle Charlie grabbed his hand and began pumping it up and down.

"It took you to do it!" he shouted. "I've spent the last fifty years looking and never been able to find any. Now you come up and find gold your first day— in the gizzard of a duck! Maybe it's a good sign."

Suddenly Velik stopped prancing and sniffed the air. Then he dashed back to the stove and began stirring.

Uncle Charlie rocked back on his heels and roared with laughter.

"Gold makes everyone forget everything. When the gold bug bites, you never get over it."

"Uncle Charlie," Barney couldn't wait any longer. "Is the gold I discovered worth anything?"

"Well, Barney," Uncle Charlie rubbed his chin and thought a minute. "It's genuine gold. There just isn't enough of it to be worth more than about"—he looked at the little cluster of nuggets—"about ninety-seven cents, I'd say."

Ninety-seven cents!

Barney was disappointed. He would have to find a lot more gold than that if he was going to be a real prospector.

Uncle Charlie picked up the duck.

"Here, Velik, you'd better get this duck cooking." He handed the gizzard to the Eskimo cook. "And don't forget this. It will probably be the most valuable gizzard we'll ever eat."

By now Barney had forgotten all about eating.

"Tell me about your looking for gold, Uncle Charlie," he coaxed.

They went into the front room.

Uncle Charlie settled himself in a comfortable chair.

"To begin with, everyone knows there's gold in this

part of the country but we've never been able to find any in large amounts. If we only knew the spot where this duck ate its last meal, we might make a real gold strike."

Uncle Charlie told of his prospecting around Unalakleet for the last fifty years. It was a thrilling story.

"At least, we know of a lot of places where there *isn't* any gold," he finished.

Velik came to the door. "Food ready!"

All at once Barney realized he was very, very hungry.

There was delicious cabbage, cornbread, fruit, cookies and, of course, the duck whose gizzard had been full of gold. Barney ate until he had to let his belt out a notch.

"Why, this is just like food we have at home—only it tastes better up here."

"It's the good Alaskan air. Makes a man hungry. You'll have to eat a lot to be tough enough to go prospecting for gold. Here," Uncle Charlie handed Barney the gold nuggets he had found in the duck gizzard. "That's the first gold you found in Alaska. I hope it won't be the last!"

Barney took the nuggets and very carefully wrapped

them in a piece of tissue paper. Long after Uncle
Charlie had put out the lamps and they had gone to
bed, he kept thinking of gold. When he went to sleep,
he dreamed of finding gold nuggets as big as base-
balls. The gold bug had really bitten him!

3

THE LAST BOAT

"Vic! Vic! Vic come!"

Barney was awakened by shouts and the sound of people running. He bounded out of bed and ran to the window. A number of Eskimos were racing down toward the beach. They were all pointing and yelling. Barney dressed quickly and hurried into the kitchen.

"What's all the excitement?" he asked Uncle Charlie who was standing before a mirror by the window, shaving.

"The ship's been sighted."

The ship! That must be the one bringing winter

supplies Uncle Charlie had told him about yesterday.
How he'd like to help with the unloading, but today
was to be his first day at school with the Eskimos.

"Will they still be unloading when school's out?"
Barney asked hopefully.

"There's no school today. When the supply ship
comes in, everybody turns out to help bring in freight.
We call it lightering."

"Gee, then I can help too, can't I?" Barney said
excitedly. "What can I do?"

"Well, the first thing is to eat a big breakfast. You'll
have a hard day ahead."

Uncle Charlie dished up plates heaped with ham,
eggs and hotcakes. Barney had no trouble at all eating his clean.

"Better have a look now and see how close the
ship is."

Uncle Charlie pushed his chair away and walked
to the window in the front room. He picked up a pair
of field glasses.

"There she is, Barney, the good ship *Vic,* loaded
with winter supplies for Unalakleet. Back in the old
days she would have been full of men coming up to
hunt for gold."

Barney looked. The ship was just a tiny spot on the horizon.

"It doesn't look close to me."

"Well, no, but the ship doesn't come all the way in to unload. The water is so shallow here, she has to anchor and unload about three miles off-shore."

"Unload off shore?" Barney wasn't sure he had heard right. "How do they do that?"

"The goods are unloaded onto big barges. I have two of them. They hold about a hundred tons each."

"But how do you get the barges out to the ship?"

"I've a tugboat just for that purpose. If you want to, you can go with me when we take out the first barge."

"Do I want to! When do we leave?"

"Not for a while yet. The tide's not right. We'll have to wait till the water gets deeper or we might get stuck on a sand bar. But there's plenty to do in the meantime." Uncle Charlie took his cap off the hook, handed Barney his jacket and they went downstairs.

"Barney, this is Paneok. He clerks in the Post."

Barney reached over the counter and shook hands with the young Eskimo.

"I don't think there's any need to keep the Post open today," Uncle Charlie said to Paneok, "everyone'll be busy lightering. Suppose you go to the warehouse and clear out a place for the new supplies."

Just as Paneok started out the front door, a man came in.

"Hello, Tagiak, I'm glad you've come. Barney, this is my other clerk. He has a team of nine white matched dogs. He's also postmaster of Unalakleet."

Tagiak grinned. "No post office today," he said.

"That's right. I want you to make a list of our work crew. We'll need about eight husky fellows to go out on the first barge and help unload the ship. Then, I'll need a crew of about twenty to work on the dock."

Barney was almost bursting with eagerness.

"What am I going to do, Uncle Charlie?"

"You'll go out to the ship with me and when we come back, with the loaded barge, you can check supplies as they're taken off."

"Swell!"

They walked to the back door of the Post and came into a big store room. Behind this was another storeroom and behind that a third.

"Gee, this place is a lot bigger than I thought," Barney exclaimed.

"It has to be big to hold the winter supplies for the village."

At last they came out of the storage rooms to the bank of the Unalakleet River. They found men, women and children all bustling around laying a wooden runway from the dock to the Trading Post.

Paneok came up. "Warehouse cleared," he reported.

"Good," Uncle Charlie squinted at the waterline on the river bank. "The tide should be about right now. Let's head out to the ship."

After one of the barges was made fast behind the tug, Paneok, Barney, Uncle Charlie and his crew of eight men went aboard.

As they left the river mouth for open sea, the tug started to bob up and down. Uncle Charlie came over to where Barney was standing by the rail.

"How are your sea legs?"

"Great!" Barney liked the gentle rocking motion and the feel of the fresh salt air on his face.

"Looks as if you're going to be a real sailor!"

The tug nosed up to the *Victoria*. From where Barney stood, the big ship looked about three stories high. Suddenly, there was a yell, then some lines came sailing through the air to land on the barge with a thump. Uncle Charlie's crew quickly secured the barge.

A voice boomed from the deck above them. "Come aboard, Charlie!"

"Hello, Captain Whitcomb!" Uncle Charlie shouted back.

A rope ladder was let down the side of the *Vic.*

"Steady now, Barney, you head up first. When the waves lift us, jump for the ladder and up you go."

Barney waited, then with a grab caught the rope ladder. He didn't dare look down as he scrambled up. A pair of strong hands pulled him over the ship's rail.

Captain Whitcomb looked surprised.

"Well, well, who's the lad?"

By this time Uncle Charlie had climbed up.

"This is my nephew, Barney, Captain. He's staying with me for the winter."

"That's good, Charlie, I'm glad you're going to have company this winter. It won't do you any harm to have some extra help at the Post either."

"Barney'll be a big help. He'll be staying from freeze-up through break-up."

"You don't say!" Captain Whitcomb exclaimed. "Sounds as if you're going to make him a real Alaskan Sourdough."

"That's right," Uncle Charlie nodded and grinned at Barney. "What's more, he's already made his first strike—found gold in the gizzard of a duck we had for dinner last night."

Captain Whitcomb looked sharply at Uncle Charlie. "Where did that duck come from, Charlie?"

"That's what we don't know, but you can bet we're going to try and find out. Maybe Barney has brought us luck."

"Well, I hope you hit it. You certainly deserve the best."

They all walked over to the open hold of the freighter.

"My men are getting your freight out now," the Captain told Uncle Charlie.

Barney looked down two decks below. He could see the ship's crew piling cartons on to a wooden platform. At a signal, this was raised by a steam winch. Everyone stopped to watch the load as it was drawn up. It began spinning and swinging dangerously back and forth, the cables creaked, the winch chugged harder. Barney hardly breathed, he was so afraid the cables might break and the load come crashing down on all of them. Slowly, the platform swung out over the ship's rail and was lowered down to the barge where Uncle Charlie's crew unloaded it. Barney breathed a sigh of relief. By this time, the men in the hold were busy with the next load.

"Well, I guess there's enough to keep the men busy for some time." Captain Whitcomb turned to Uncle Charlie. "Let's go to my cabin and have some coffee while we look over your cargo list."

"Right you are, Captain. Do you want to come along, Barney?"

Barney looked at another load of freight soaring into the air. This was much too exciting to leave.

"I'd like to stay here and watch, Uncle Charlie, if that's all right."

"Sure, that'll be fine," Uncle Charlie and Captain Whitcomb disappeared into a cabin.

There were a lot of interesting things to see.

First Paneok left with the tug to bring back the second barge.

Then there were all the different shaped cartons and crates the men in the hold kept piling up. Bar-

ney tried to imagine what each one contained and
as the load swung over his head, he would look for
a stamp or label on the outside telling him if he
were right or wrong.

There was a red-haired fellow named Big Jim.
The muscles in his arms looked big as footballs. He
stood by the ship's rail and signalled to the winch
operator when to raise the load, swing over and
lower it.

Big Jim's job must be very important, Barney decided, one mistake and the whole load might be
spilled.

Once during the morning the loaders stopped working to have coffee. They invited Uncle Charlie's crew
aboard and right there, before Barney's eyes, the eight
men stepped onto the loading platform and, holding
fast to the cables, were hoisted aboard.

A little later, Barney saw the tug coming out with
the second barge. Paneok eased it in, then came around
front to pick up the loaded barge.

"That's it, men!" Big Jim called. "That's all she'll
hold. Time to start on the next one." He motioned to
Barney, "Want to go tell your Uncle his barge is
loaded? He's in the first cabin on the right."

"Sure," Barney agreed and went to Captain Whitcomb's cabin.

"The barge is loaded," he announced coming in the door.

"Then, that's our signal to get underway, Barney," Uncle Charlie looked up from the lists he and the Captain had been checking.

They all hurried out on deck. Uncle Charlie peered down at the loaded barge. "Well, I guess we're ready to take off."

He and Barney shook hands with Captain Whitcomb, then climbed down the rope ladder to the tug. Lines were cast off.

"See you next spring, Barney," Captain Whitcomb called as the tug pulled away and started for shore.

Back at the dock, the Eskimos were waiting with freight carts, wheelbarrows and strong, willing arms.

Barney stood on the dock and checked freight as it came off the barge. Except for a half-hour break for lunch, they worked all afternoon unloading cartons of canned foods and canned milk. Around dinner time, Velik came out with sandwiches and coffee for everyone. Then they worked on until nine o'clock when the second barge came in loaded with more

canned goods, sacks of potatoes and drums of oil and
gasoline. Barney was making his figures by lamplight
and getting very tired. His job wasn't easy. Some of
the freight was missing, some of the orders were short
and a few of the cartons and crates were broken.
All of this had to be noted. Barney hadn't dreamed
that it took so much to keep an Eskimo village through
the winter.

Uncle Charlie came up, "How're you doing?"

"All right, I guess," Barney straightened up so Unc
wouldn't see how tired he was.

"We'll work till midnight, then call it quits. The
empty barge won't be able to go out to the ship until
early morning when the tide changes."

They stopped half-way through the second barge
around eleven thirty. Uncle Charlie and Barney went
up to the kitchen.

"Tired?" Uncle Charlie asked.

"A little," Barney admitted.

"This is a hard time for everyone. We all have to
be on the go day and night. If a storm came up we
might not be able to unload our winter supplies and
that would be too bad for all of us. Are you hungry?"

"Hungry as a bear."

"You mean a Polar bear," Uncle Charlie joked.
"Remember, you're up north now." He went to the
stove and fried up some ham and eggs. They tasted
almost as good as the bed felt when Barney at last
tumbled in.

It seemed to Barney he had just gone to sleep when
Uncle Charlie was shaking his shoulder next morning.

"Wake up, Barney! It looks stormy. We have to
get that barge unloaded."

"What time is it?" Barney asked sleepily.

"About five. Time for all good Alaskans to be up
and about!"

Five in the morning and he'd just gone to bed at
twelve!

"That's the way of the North," Uncle Charlie told
him at breakfast. "There are times when you have to
work double, but to make up for it there are times
when you get double doses of rest."

"When's that?" Barney wanted to know, hoping
Uncle Charlie would say, "soon."

"When the blizzards come. No one goes out then
unless absolutely necessary. You just stay inside where
it's warm."

Down at the dock, the Eskimos were all ready.

Everyone pitched in and by noon the second barge was unloaded. Then, they started in on the third loaded with coal and lumber. Everyone hurried. The sky was getting darker and darker with storm clouds. Velik brought sandwiches in mid-afternoon. Barney was glad for a rest. His head was beginning to swim from counting freight and watching the Eskimos leave and return ready to go again. Eskimo women, some with their babies tied snugly on their backs, lifted and hauled as much cargo as anyone else.

There was one big bright spot in all the work. Anagik was helping unload. Every time he came down with his cart, he grinned at Barney. Once he stopped a minute.

"You going to school here?" he asked.

Barney nodded. "Yes, I am."

"I'll come by for you, then. I'll imitate a ptarmigan. Like this," Anagik made a sort of whirring noise.

"I'll listen for it," Barney told him. Then they both went back to work.

"This is the last load," Uncle Charlie said pointing to the fourth barge to be pulled in by the tug. It was around eight at night.

"I'm glad of that," Barney said and meant it. The sky looked stormier than ever. A rain would ruin the cement, flour and bolts of cloth on the last barge. These were the first things to be taken off, then ammunition, hardware, and crates of eggs.

Barney had just jumped to the barge to check some of the load when he heard a shout. One of the men had caught the wheel of his freight cart on the side of the runway. The whole load toppled over and down the ten feet to the beach.

Uh-oh! thought Barney. I hope there weren't any eggs on that load!

He rushed down the gangway where the load had spilled. There were no crates of broken eggs but one of the cardboard cartons was split and several pans had fallen out.

"What's this?" Uncle Charlie asked, coming up, "what happened?"

"One of the freight carts went over," Barney explained. "No damage, just a few pans spilled. Say, those are funny looking pans, what are they used for?"

"For panning gold, Barney. One of them is yours."

Panning gold! Barney would like to have asked

Uncle Charlie more about that but he had to get back to his post. He put the questions he would ask in the back of his mind to be brought out at the very first chance.

By three o'clock in the morning, all of the barges had been emptied. A cold rain was beginning to fall but it didn't matter. All of the freight was safely in the storerooms of the Trading Post. They'd won their race with the storm!

Barney was dead tired. He dragged upstairs behind Uncle Charlie. They both dropped into chairs and didn't stir for several minutes. Finally Uncle Charlie said, "You did a fine job, Barney."

"I never worked so hard in all my life."

"Yes, and I'm proud of you. You'll have plenty to eat this winter and so will the villagers."

"Oh, I almost forgot. Has the *Vic* gone?"

"Yes, she left right after the last barge was loaded. That's the last ship you'll see till next June."

Barney rose wearily from his chair.

"Aren't you hungry?" Uncle Charlie asked.

"I'm too tired to eat, Uncle Charlie."

"Good. I'm too tired to fix anything. Let's go to bed. I think we deserve a rest."

Barney walked slowly to his door, then he turned back, "You say there won't be any more boats till next June?"

"That's right."

"It's a good thing. The way I feel, it'll take that long to rest up."

"Think you'll be too tired to go to school with the Eskimos tomorrow?" Uncle Charlie asked slyly.

Barney decided he wasn't as tired as he thought.

"Of course not," he said stoutly. "Will I be able to understand what they're talking about?"

"Oh, sure, the teachers all teach in English and the children all speak it."

Barney was relieved.

"Anagik's coming by for me."

"Good! He's a fine boy."

"Then you wake me at seven," Barney told Uncle Charlie. He wanted to be ready when he heard the whir of a ptarmigan.

4

SCHOOL WITH THE ESKIMOS

Barney stopped with his last bite of ham and eggs half way to his mouth. He'd heard the whir of a ptarmigan outside the kitchen window!

"Have to go now," he jumped up, grabbed up his jacket and was two leaps down the steps before he remembered his manners.

"Excuse me," he yelled back.

"That's all right, Barney. Run along to school," Uncle Charlie called after him.

There were so many things Barney wanted to ask Anagik. Did they play football up here? Did Anagik have a dog team? And, of course, Barney wanted to tell Anagik about discovering gold in the duck gizzard. Maybe Anagik had even been prospecting!

Barney stepped out into the crisp morning air. His Eskimo friend was waiting.

"Hi, Anagik!"

"Hello, Barney."

"Am I late?" Barney was anxious to know.

"No. We've plenty of time. School's right over there," Anagik pointed across the acre of bare ground in front of the Trading Post which was the village square. Barney looked at the large two-story yellow frame building.

"Uncle Charlie told me that was the school building but I haven't had time to notice it. Looks a lot like the country schools where I come from."

"Where you from?" Anagik asked. Barney told him and realized he wasn't the only one who was going to ask questions. Anagik wanted to learn just as much as he did.

"Do you play football up here?" Barney asked as they walked across the square.

Anagik nodded, "But not like football outside. We play with a round ball and try and kick it over a line. The best game is 'mah-nee, mah-nee,'" his new friend went on, "it's fun. You can be on my team."

Barney couldn't wait any longer to tell Anagik of discovering gold in the duck gizzard. When he came to the part about gold, Anagik stopped and stared.

"Where did that duck come from?" he asked.

"We don't know," Barney admitted, "but—maybe you and I can find out sometime. We might go prospecting—"

"Swell," Anagik agreed enthusiastically, "I went once with my Mother's brother. It was fun but we didn't find any gold. I have a dog team—"

Just then, the school bell began to ring. Boys and girls came running from all directions down the paths leading into the square.

Barney would like to have talked more about prospecting but by this time they'd come to the school entrance. They climbed the steps and went inside. Anagik introduced Barney to the teachers in charge. They were Mr. and Mrs. Fisher, a couple who'd come up from the States to teach the Eskimos. Mr. Fisher shook hands with Barney.

"Welcome to school in Unalakleet," he said with a broad grin. "Now I'll take you to meet your teacher."

Barney followed Mr. Fisher into a classroom that looked just like his homeroom back in Porterville. There were the same kind of desks and a blackboard. There was a rack of maps on the wall and a border around the blackboard decorated with colored drawings.

Barney looked to the front of the room and saw his teacher, an Eskimo woman. Mr. Fisher explained that Miss Royluk had gone to school out in the States and come back to teach her people.

Miss Royluk looked over the room for a seat for Barney. Anagik pointed to an empty desk right across the aisle from him. Miss Royluk looked at Anagik, then she looked at Barney.

"I think you two boys would do better work if I put Barney right here," she walked over to a desk all the way across the room from Anagik.

"School teachers aren't any different up here," Barney decided as he took his place.

School started off with a salute to the American flag. Then, Miss Royluk asked Barney to point out on the United States map where he lived and this started off the geography lesson.

Barney found out that both the 6th and 7th grades

had this room and were taught by Miss Royluk. All of the boys and girls were smaller than himself. Barney had noticed their parents weren't as big as people in the United States either. The subjects were just the same as the 7th grade in Porterville and Barney was just as glad as he'd always been in school at home when recess came.

Once outside, Anagik took Barney by the arm,

"Come on, we have to hurry to play mah-nee, mah-nee before the bell rings."

One team had already lined up at the far side of the square. Anagik's team was waiting impatiently for him to come so they could start.

Mah-nee, mah-nee was a lot like Prisoner's Base. Each team tried to cross the middle of the square which was "no man's land" to a safety zone at the other side. It was an exciting game with everyone running hard and some of the pupils who didn't play standing on the sidelines cheering and yelling.

When Barney stopped once to catch his breath, he saw a bunch of boys standing in a circle watching something. 'Must be a fight,' he thought, and went over. Since he was taller than anyone else, he could see. There in the center were two boys. They were sitting on the ground facing each other with the middle fingers of their right hands linked. At a signal, each one would try to pull the other toward himself. They pulled very hard. Barney could hear them breathing in loud grunts. Finally, one of the boys succeeded in pulling the other over to his side. Everyone laughed and clapped and two other boys sat down to try their luck.

"What're they playing?" Barney whispered to a boy in front of him.

"Finger pull," he said, "would you like to try?"

"Yes," Barney answered, then he remembered mah-nee, mah-nee, "but I'm playing something else. I'll have to try finger pull later."

Barney was sorry when recess was over but classes went fast the rest of the morning. There was arithmetic and he always liked that. When noon came, everyone was served with plate lunches of fresh cabbage salad, turnips, potatoes and a cup of canned milk. Barney picked up his plate and went over to the desk across from Anagik.

"Mmmmm, this food tastes good," he said after the first bite.

"I grew the cabbage in my garden and sold it to the

school," Anagik said. "I raise all sorts of vegetables." "You do!" Barney exclaimed. "I didn't know there were fresh vegetables up here."

"Sure. Everyone has gardens in the summer. Those potatoes and turnips were grown here too."

Barney ate every bite of his food but wasn't able to drink more than half the canned milk which was mixed with water. He felt guilty leaving any after he learned the government furnished this lunch to students for only ten cents.

When lunch was finished, Barney asked if they would play mah-nee, mah-nee again.

"We could—or we could do something else."

Anagik looked very mysterious.

"What else?" Barney wondered what could be more fun than mah-nee, mah-nee.

Anagik bent across the aisle and talked close to Barney's ear so no one else would hear.

"Promise you won't tell anyone," he began. Barney promised.

"Every day at noon, I go off by myself and practice the double kick."

"What's the double kick?"

"You kick at a ball hanging in front of you with

both feet at the same time," Anagik explained. This sounded impossible to Barney.

"But why do you practice by yourself?" Barney asked lowering his voice.

"Because," Anagik looked around to make sure no one was listening, "there's a double kick contest every New Year's. There has been for a long time. My Father used to be in it and he was champion for six years straight and two times after that. He was finally beaten by Mayuk's father. That's Mayuk over there," Anagik pointed to a boy in the front seat of the fourth row. "Now this year, Mayuk is going to enter the double kick contest and I want to beat him."

Barney looked at Mayuk. He was taller than Anagik but not heavy.

"He looks taller than you," Barney whispered, "will that make any difference?"

"Yes, his legs are longer than mine," Anagik said glumly. "That's why I'm practicing."

"I'd like to go with you," Barney told his friend.

"Good! I'll teach you how to double kick. Then, maybe if I don't beat Mayuk, you will."

They went outside and Anagik led Barney over behind a cabin where no one would see them, then he showed Barney how to double kick. Barney was very clumsy. It was hard for him to bring both feet up at the same time. Once he sat down hard on the ground.

"I'm afraid you'll have to beat Mayuk yourself," he told Anagik as they walked back to their classroom.

"You'll learn," Anagik assured him, "you have long legs too."

The rest of the day flew by. When school was over and Barney and Anagik came out the door, the air was much colder.

"A-la-pah!" Anagik exclaimed.

"What?" Barney didn't understand.

"That means cold," Anagik told him. "Look," he pointed to a whirling windcharger, "the northwind's starting to blow. Freeze-up's getting near."

Barney turned up his jacket collar and shoved his hands deep into his pockets. If it's this cold tomorrow, I'll wear my fur clothes, he thought to himself.

He and Anagik walked down toward the beach. A group of men were bending over an oblong white object.

"What's that?" Barney asked.

"White whale," Anagik told him, "they're cutting it up. Want to go down and watch?"

Barney nodded. They walked over to the men. As they watched, Anagik told Barney about whale hunting. Some were caught in nets but this one had been shot. Anagik pointed to one little hole over the whale's eye.

"This beluga was killed with one bullet. Towark shot it from an outboard motor boat."

Towark must be a good shot to kill a moving whale from a moving boat, Barney decided.

By now, several women had showed up with pans and kettles. Each of them began gathering up the big squares of thick skin cut off the white whale.

"Those are the wives of the hunters," Anagik went on, "but anyone who wants to can get a piece of beluga while it's being cut up. Once it's put in the cache, the hunter doesn't have to give any more away."

Barney noticed a man carving off one of the flippers.

"Look, Anagik, that man's carving off a flipper. Is he going to use *that*?"

"Yep. That man's Towark and he gets the flipper

because he's the one that killed the whale. The flipper's the best part."

Towark looked up. When he saw the boys, he smiled and held the flipper out to Barney.

"Want a bite?" he invited.

Barney's mouth dropped open. Eat the flipper of a whale raw!

"Go ahead, and take a bite," Anagik urged, "it's good."

Barney took a small sliver Towark sliced off for him and with a deep gulp, bit off a piece. It didn't taste bad at all. In fact, it tasted good! It had a nutty flavor but it was awfully tough. Barney chewed and chewed. The hunters all stood around and grinned at Barney while he chewed with all his might.

Just then, who should come up but Uncle Charlie. All the men turned to say hello. Quickly, Barney slipped what was left of the flipper out of his mouth, then he turned to Uncle Charlie.

"Hello," Uncle Charlie said, "I didn't expect to find you down here."

Barney explained that he and Anagik had been watching the men cut up Towark's beluga.

"Were you looking for me?" he asked. He hadn't

realized it was getting late until just this minute.

"Nope, I figure you can take care of yourself. I was just going down to the river mouth to see if there's any sign of slush ice yet."

"Slush ice?"

"Yes, that's the first sign of freeze-up. Want to come along?"

Barney said good-bye to Anagik and the men. As he walked with Uncle Charlie he told of his day in school and of chewing the whale flipper and getting rid of it. He was very careful not to mention about Anagik and him practicing the double kick.

When they came to the river, Uncle Charlie pointed out grey masses of ice floating on the water.

"That's slush ice, Barney. The creeks in the hills are starting to freeze."

Barney looked closely. He guessed slush ice was called that because it looked just like snow which had turned to slush. All at once, Barney realized he was cold. The wind was cutting through his jacket as if he didn't have one on. He shivered.

"What's the matter? Cold?" Uncle Charlie asked.

Barney nodded. He couldn't keep his teeth from chattering.

"Then, we'll head back." They started walking along the river toward the Trading Post. "I found some gold right here once," Uncle Charlie stopped and kicked at the soft sand bank.

"You did!" Barney hurried over and peered at the spot as if he still expected to see some gold.

"Yes, that's where you find gold—in the creek beds where the water's washed the soil away."

"Did you find much gold?"

"No, just a few small grains, but there's gold around here somewhere—we're all sure of that."

Barney looked up and down the river bank. Someday *he* would prospect on that bank. Maybe *he* would find the gold they all knew was there.

"When can I go prospecting, Uncle Charlie?"

"Well, let's see now," Uncle Charlie paused, "I expect it will be all right for you to go when you're a Sourdough. By that time you'll know what to do out on trail."

"Sourdough! What's that?" Barney asked. He remembered hearing Captain Whitcomb and Uncle Charlie mention it.

"Why, that's what the men were called who came up in the big gold rush to Alaska in 1898. Nowadays, that's what we call a Real Alaskan."

"What do you have to do to be a Sourdough?" Barney began walking backwards so the wind didn't hit his face.

"Well, Barney, the main thing you have to do is live through an Alaskan winter from freeze-up till after break-up in the spring."

"Oh," Barney's face fell, "then I can't go prospecting till spring?"

"That's right but I don't think you'll have any trouble keeping busy until then." Uncle Charlie blew on his hands. "Say, it *is* getting cold. Freeze-up's certainly not far off now."

Maybe freeze-up will come tomorrow, Barney thought to himself. If that happened he would be half a Sourdough already and half a prospector too!

5

FREEZE-UP

Barney went to the pencil sharpener on the window ledge for about the eighth time and looked hopefully toward the river mouth. It had been two days since he'd gone to bed sure freeze-up would come.

"If the whole year goes this slow, I'll never get to be a Sourdough and go prospecting," he thought mournfully.

The northwind blew most of the time but although more and more ice choked the river, it remained open. A little snow had fallen the night after the northwind began to blow but not enough for dog sledding. Still it was cold enough for Barney to wear his fur parka and boots all the time now.

The first time he'd worn them Anagik took him out on the tundra after school and showed him a special kind of grass to stuff in the soles of his boots to make them warmer. While out, they'd seen several Eskimos gathering huge bunches of grass.

"What're they pulling so much grass for, Anagik? They won't need all that for boots, will they?"

"No, Barney, they're getting in a supply for their dogs to sleep on."

Later that afternoon, the boys had gone down to the river to watch for freeze-up. They'd gone again this morning and at noon. Anagik was just as anxious for the river to be covered with ice as Barney because he wanted to get his dogs out for a run. Barney stood at the window thinking how much fun it would be to go out with Anagik and his team—or better still with his own team.

"Barney!!" his day dreaming was cut short. It was Miss Royluk. "Don't you think your pencil is sharp enough now?"

"Yes Ma'm," Barney answered meekly. He hadn't even sharpened it because it was still sharp from his other visits to the window.

"And you try to make this point do for the rest of the day," Miss Royluk added.

"Yes Ma'm," Barney looked over at Anagik. His friend knew why he kept going to the window. Anagik raised his eyebrows asking Barney with his eyes if the freeze-up had come. Barney shook his head ever so slightly.

At last school was out. They both raced down to the river mouth. Great round flat sections of ice filled the river.

"Pancake ice," Anagik told him. Barney looked. They really did look like giant pancakes with the edges curled up.

Parts of the river were already frozen. In places where it was still open, the ice was so thick the water hardly moved at all. Ice was filling the Bering Sea.

Barney and Anagik started walking up the coast. Several old women and little children were gathering driftwood from the beach for fuel during the winter.

"There's Kyrok. Let's go over and see her." Anagik started toward an old woman wearing a bright red cloth-covered parka.

"Hello, Kyrok. This is my friend, Barney."

The old woman stopped her work a minute. She smiled at Barney and held out her hand.

"Yah, yah!" she said.

"Kyrok doesn't speak English," Anagik explained. "Not many of the old Eskimos do. She's saying welcome."

After Barney had shaken hands, Kyrok and Anagik talked for a few minutes in Eskimo. Then Anagik turned to Barney.

"O.K. Let's go."

"What were you talking about?" Barney asked as they waved good-bye and walked away.

"Oh, I offered to help her gather firewood but she told me she didn't need any help. She'll only carry the little sticks home and leave the large pieces for her grandson to get with his dog sled."

"You mean she'll leave her stack of firewood out on the beach? Won't anyone steal it?"

"Nope. Nobody will disturb anyone's firewood on the beach once it's stacked," Anagik said positively. "I have to go home now and check over my dog harnesses. Some of them need patching. Want to come with me?"

"Gee, I'd like to, Anagik, but I can't," Barney told his friend. "I guess it's time I was getting back to the Trading Post to fill the lamps before supper." It was Barney's job to clean the lamps and fill them with gasoline every night.

"Well, solong, then," Anagik looked toward the river and out to Sea once more. "It oughtn't to be long before freeze-up now, for sure. If it comes, I'll have my dogs out tomorrow. I want to get them in shape for our prospecting next spring. You can go with me if you want to."

Did he want to? Barney couldn't think of anything he'd rather do!

"Swell!" then he remembered he was to work at the Trading Post on Saturdays, "only I'll have to go after the Post closes tomorrow afternoon. Will that be all right?"

"Sure, I'll come by for you. Bye."

"Good-bye, Anagik."

Barney almost ran all the way to the Trading Post, he was so excited thinking about going out with Anagik and his team.

Back at the Post, Tagiak was busy building a fire in the basement storeroom. Paneok was filling the barrels in the kitchen to the brim with water.

"That may be the last water we'll have for a long time without melting down ice for it," Uncle Charlie observed.

"Uncle Charlie," Barney talked as he cleaned the lamps, "Anagik says if freeze-up comes tonight, he'll take his dogs out tomorrow. Can I go with him after the Post closes?"

"Sure," Uncle Charlie said, "only you want to be careful. Even after the river freezes over, the ice may not be strong enough for dog sleds for a day or two."

"But I'll be half a Sourdough, the minute the river is covered with ice, won't I?" Barney asked hopefully, "even before the ice is thick enough for dog sleds?"

Uncle Charlie laughed.

"That you will, Barney. And judging by the looks of things, you should certainly be half a Sourdough by tomorrow morning."

Half a Sourdough! Half a "real Alaskan." Sourdough! That was a funny thing to call a real Alaskan.

"Sourdough's a queer name, Uncle Charlie, where'd it come from?"

"That's a good question, Barney. All the prospectors back in the Gold Rush days of '98 carried some sour dough with them to make pancakes and bread from. They'd save a little back every day to start the next day's batch from. That's how they got the name—because they always had some sour dough with them."

"Well, for Pete's sake!" Barney exclaimed, "I'd never have guessed that. How does sour dough taste, Uncle Charlie?"

"It tastes good. But you ought to know that. You've been eating flapjacks made from sour dough ever since you've been here."

Barney was certainly surprised. He'd thought the pancakes were mighty good but he didn't dream they were any special kind like sour dough ones.

After supper that night Barney went straight to bed. Tomorrow was going to be a big day and he didn't want to sleep any more of it away than he could help.

He awoke before he heard anyone moving about in the kitchen. With one leap, he was at the window. Even in the pale early morning light he could see that the river was at last completely frozen over.

Freeze-up had come! Barney was now *half a sour-dough! Halfway to prospecting!*

He hurried into his fur boots, trousers and parka and tiptoed into the kitchen. No one was stirring. Barney went down the stairs very quietly—it wasn't hard to do with his fur boots—then he slipped outside. Once out of the Trading Post, he broke into a run to the river bank.

The village was very quiet. Here and there, a few lamps showed through the windows but no one was outside.

Yes, the river was really frozen over from bank to bank. Barney gazed out toward the Sea and couldn't believe what he saw. The Bering Sea was frozen over too for about a mile and a half out!

He looked back at the river.

Wonder how thick that ice really is, he thought to himself. He climbed down the bank for a closer look but he couldn't tell. He could see the dark water of the river underneath as clear as if he were looking through glass. It might be one inch and it might be one foot for all Barney knew. Was the ice thick enough to hold a dog team. That was the question that kept pounding through Barney's head.

He carefully put one foot on the ice. Nothing happened. The ice held. He stamped his foot up and down. The ice felt as firm as a board. Then Barney brought the other foot on to the ice. Nothing happened. He took a step, then another and another. He walked out to the center of the river.

This ice is thick enough for a dog sled, Barney told himself gleefully. Then he remembered the place where the river had still been open yesterday. Now I'll go over to try that, he decided, feeling very important. He walked toward the spot. He hadn't taken more than three steps when he heard a sharp crack. Barney didn't need to be told what it was. All around him he heard the ice cracking. At the same moment he began to feel the ice under him give way. Barney was so frightened, he couldn't move. His heart came up in his mouth. Just then a sharp command rang out in the morning air:

"Lie flat! Lie flat! Lie down on ice."

Without even thinking, Barney threw himself down on the ice.

"Crawl on stomach. Come on. Crawl toward bank," the voice ordered again.

Barney started inching across the ice. He was so

scared he didn't even look to see who was directing him. It seemed like ages before he reached the river bank, his body wet with sweat. He looked up. A sturdy, keen-eyed Eskimo stood on top of the bank.

"Here, grab ice pick," the man let down one end of a long pole. Barney grabbed the ice pick just above its sharp ivory point and was pulled up the bank. His knees wobbled so badly he could hardly stand.

The man stared at Barney with disapproval. Finally, he spoke:

"My name Achebuk."

"My name's Barney," Barney's voice shook a little. He wasn't over being scared yet. "You saved my life."

Achebuk said nothing. He just stood and looked Barney straight in the eye. Barney felt ashamed of himself.

"I guess I shouldn't have gone out on the ice," he began.

"Ice dangerous. Eskimo always test with ice pick before walking on it," Achebuk's voice was stern.

"I was just trying to find out if the ice was strong enough for dog sleds," Barney tried to explain.

Achebuk turned and began to walk away. Once he looked back.

"Ice dangerous," he said again and disappeared around a cabin.

Barney started toward the Trading Post. Uncle Charlie was very surprised to see him walk into the kitchen.

"Why, I thought you were still in bed asleep!" he said in surprise. "How long have you been up?"

"Oh for some time," Barney said trying to act as if nothing at all had happened.

"Well," Uncle Charlie smiled, "I guess you know you're now half a Sourdough."

"Yes, Sir."

"And I suppose you're all set to go for a dog sled ride today with Anagik?"

"Well," Barney hesitated, "maybe. Of course," he added wisely, "Anagik and I'll have to test the ice with an ice pick first to make sure it's strong enough."

Uncle Charlie looked up from his plate. He was so surprised he put down his coffee cup without taking a sip.

"Great Christopher!" he exclaimed. "You certainly catch on fast for just being half a Sourdough. One

of the first things to learn up here is respect for the
ice. Looks like you've learned that already and here
I thought I'd have a Cheechako on my hands this
winter."

"Cheechako! What's that?"

"That's the word for a greenhorn, a new comer
to Alaska who doesn't know how to get along."

Barney sat back in his chair. Should he tell Uncle
Charlie about getting caught on the ice. He guessed
he should but still it was nice having Uncle Charlie
think he was so smart. Before he could make up his
mind, Uncle Charlie was going over the things Barney was to do in the Trading Post.

"The first thing every Saturday morning is to turn
the eggs."

"Turn the eggs?" Barney didn't understand.

"Yep, those crates of eggs which came in on the
Vic have to be turned every few days to keep them
from spoiling. We'll be eating them till next summer,
you know."

Barney went down to the cellar storage and turned
the eggs. It took a long time for there were a lot of
crates. While he was working, he kept arguing with
himself whether or not to let Uncle Charlie know

he really wasn't as smart as he'd pretended—that he really was a Cheechako.

After the eggs had been turned, Barney filled the oil barrels for the kitchen stove and the stove in his room. Then he went out to split some wood. While he was stacking the chopped wood, Anagik came up.

"Hello, Barney, did you know freeze-up came last night?"

"Yep, I knew," Barney replied driving his ax into the chopping block.

"I'm just going down to the river to see if the ice is thick enough for my dog sled."

"The ice isn't thick enough, Anagik," Barney declared.

"Why, Barney, how do you know?" Anagik looked surprised.

Then Barney told Anagik about what had happened and how Achebuk had saved his life.

"I don't think Achebuk thought much of me," Barney finished.

"I guess Achebuk would be a little disgusted at that," Anagik admitted. "You see, he's the best seal hunter in the village and he knows how dangerous ice can really be."

"Aw Gee!" Now Barney was as disgusted with himself as Achebuk probably was. The best seal hunter in the village and he'd seen Barney do a very foolish thing! Barney leaned against the side of the Trading Post. He gazed at the fur tips of his boots and thought how dumb he had acted.

"Well, Barney," Anagik broke the silence, "guess I'll have to go. Maybe the ice'll be strong enough for the dog sled tomorrow."

"Yeah," Barney answered but he wasn't thinking about going out with Anagik's team tomorrow. He was thinking what he'd say to Uncle Charlie at lunch.

He carried the wood in and went upstairs to eat. They had just pulled their chairs up to the table and Barney was thinking how he would start when someone knocked at the door of the kitchen.

"Come in," Uncle Charlie called.

It was Nipchuk, the Eskimo who'd brought Barney the duck with the gold in its gizzard.

"Hello, Nipchuk. Say we've a good story to tell you. Sit down." Then Uncle Charlie told Nipchuk all about Barney's discovering gold. The Eskimo's eyes began to shine. When Uncle Charlie had finished, he edged forward in his chair.

"Want me to look for gold for you, Traeger? I know good place to prospect."

"Where?" now Uncle Charlie leaned forward.

"At old reindeer camp down coast. About twenty miles. I find signs of gold there last year." Barney listened very closely. Gold that close to Unalakleet!

Uncle Charlie sat back in his chair and rubbed his chin.

"Mmmmmm," he was thinking hard.

"You stake me for winter, I give you half," the Eskimo continued.

Uncle Charlie made up his mind.

"All right, Nipchuk, I'll stake you to your grub for the winter. Maybe this time I'll hit it, by cracky!" He turned to Barney.

"You go downstairs with Nipchuk and get up his supplies. Make a list of everything."

Barney and Nipchuk went downstairs. There a lot of work to getting up a winter's grubstake. He had to get together a pick and buckets, a shovel, flour and sugar, all kinds of canned foods and ammunition. All the while he kept wishing he were going along to discover gold. Uncle Charlie came down just as he was finishing.

They both wished Nipchuk good luck and watched the Eskimo pull his supplies away on a sled. Then they went upstairs for supper. Barney kept trying to get up nerve to tell the truth to Uncle Charlie all during their meal but he couldn't do it. They went into the front room and listened to the radio. After awhile, Uncle Charlie said, "Wonder how cold it's getting," and walked over to the window to look at the thermometer. "Come here a minute, Barney," he called.

Barney went over to the open window. Uncle Charlie pointed up, "Look."

There in the dark night, Barney could see streamers of yellow and light green drifting across the sky.

"What in the world is that?" he asked in amazement.

"Those are northern lights. I guess they're celebrating your being half a Sourdough."

Barney gulped.

"Uncle Charlie, I'm really not so much a Sourdough as a Cheechako. I almost went through the ice this morning."

"You did!" Uncle Charlie looked surprised, then he started laughing, "Well, well, Barney, all that talk about testing the ice was something you just learned the hard way, wasn't it?"

"That's right," already Barney felt much better.

"But you're wrong about being more of a Cheechako than a Sourdough. Cheechakos won't admit when they're wrong and you just did."

Barney was certainly relieved.

"Is that a fact? But say, Uncle Charlie, do you think the ice will be thick enough for dog sleds tomorrow?"

"It's likely to. Northern lights mean a change in the weather and it's my guess the change will be to colder. I imagine the ice'll be about right for a dog sled ride right after Sunday School tomorrow."

6

THREE SURPRISES

Even though Barney started across the square the minute he heard the bell ring for church, he found the mission almost filled. All of the seats around the big sheet-iron stove in the center of the room were already taken, so Barney sat over by a window where he could watch the people coming to the service. It seemed as if everyone in the village was out. They all formed a big procession on the main path. Once inside, it was fun to watch mothers with babies on their backs untie the sash holding baby and slip him out just before they sat down.

Mrs. Lindgren, the missionary's wife, started pumping

on the little organ up front and the choir stood. They sang a hymn, first in English, then in Eskimo. They sing as if they really like to, Barney thought.

He sat very straight on the hard wooden bench while the Reverend Lindgren delivered his sermon. Tagiak, the postmaster, stood beside the missionary and repeated each sentence in Eskimo so the older people who didn't speak English would understand.

Once Barney stole a glimpse at Anagik. There hadn't been any chance to talk before church and there were so many plans to be made! A three-inch snow had fallen last night. Barney was sure Anagik would be taking his dog team out now. They would have to decide on a place to meet and a time to go.

Just then everyone stood up. There was a benediction and mission services were over. Barney waited for Anagik. Finally his friend came out.

"Anagik!"

"Hello, Barney."

"What time are you going to take your dogs out? Uncle Charlie said I could go with you."

Anagik looked sad. "I won't have a team of my own this year, Barney. My Uncle has come to live with us. He needed a team to go trapping so I gave him mine."

"Oh," Barney's face fell. He was awfully disappointed. It wasn't just today he was sorry about. How could they go prospecting next spring? But he didn't say anything because he knew Anagik was as sorry as he.

"I'm going to get some more puppies and start training them right away—"

"That'll be swell." Barney began to hope maybe they might go prospecting after all.

"But they won't be ready for the trail by next spring," Anagik added miserably.

"Oh," Barney was more disappointed than ever. Then, because he couldn't think of anything cheerful to say, he said he guessed he'd better be going.

"O.K. See you in school tomorrow." Anagik started toward his home. He didn't feel like talking either.

Barney walked slowly back to the Trading Post. He was very unhappy. His feet dragged through the new snow. A lot of good this snow is now, he thought impatiently. He opened the door of the Post and walked quietly upstairs. No one was around. He called. There was no answer. Barney couldn't imagine where Uncle Charlie was. Then Barney heard the door open downstairs.

"Barney!" It was Uncle Charlie.

"Yes, sir."

"Come on downstairs. I have a surprise for you."

Barney grabbed up his parka and ran downstairs. When he came out the front door, there was Uncle Charlie holding a large, white sled dog by the harness! When the dog saw Barney, he leaped forward wagging his tail.

"What a beauty!" Barney gasped. "Wherever did you get him, Uncle Charlie?"

"Well, Barney, if you really want to know, I brought him over from Paneok's. He's been staying there since the day before you arrived."

The dog looked up. Then, with a little whining yelp, he stood on his hind legs. Barney laughed.

"Not so fast there, Fellow," he said gently. The dog sat down and Barney knelt beside him rubbing his soft white fur.

"Then this dog is yours?" Barney asked Uncle Charlie.

"No, Barney, he's yours."

"Mine?" Barney whirled around. Uncle Charlie nodded.

So this was the surprise! What a wonderful one it

was. This big, beautiful white sled dog was his, all his!

"Gee, Uncle Charlie, you're certainly good to me," was all Barney could think to say.

"His name's Seegoo," Uncle Charlie told Barney. "He's a young dog but he's very smart and fast." Uncle Charlie went on to say that Seegoo had been given his name because he was born on the day freeze-up came last year. Seegoo meant ice.

While Uncle Charlie talked, Seegoo sniffed at Barney, and licked his young master's hands and face. Barney put both arms around his dog's neck.

"Looks like you two are going to get along," Uncle Charlie said.

"He's a beauty," Barney looked up, "and he likes me. I can tell. You do, don't you, Seegoo?" Seegoo burrowed his nose into Barney's parka ruff.

"I thought you and Anagik were going out dog teaming this afternoon."

"We were—only Anagik had to lend his team to his uncle," Barney explained.

"Well, I guess it's up to you to take Anagik out, then."

"Take Anagik out?" Barney echoed. "How?"

"Why with your dog team, Barney. Seegoo is the

leader. And now," Uncle Charlie started back of the Trading Post, "you'd better meet the rest of your team."

Barney was almost too astonished to get off his knees, but not for long. He scrambled up and ran after Uncle Charlie with Seegoo loping along beside him. When Barney and Seegoo came around the corner, a chorus of barks and howls met them. There, chained to posts, were two beautiful all-white dogs like Seegoo, but not quite as large. Barney stopped still in amazement. He turned to Uncle Charlie.

"Do you mean all three of these dogs are mine?"

"That's right," Uncle Charlie assured him.

"But you said *a* surprise. This makes *three* surprises."

Uncle Charlie laughed. "Three dogs make up your team. Three surprises make one big surprise."

Barney went over to pet them.

"Let the dogs sniff your hand first so they'll get to know you. When they lick your hand you'll know you can start to pet them," Uncle Charlie said.

Barney held out his hand for the two dogs to sniff. Seegoo was by his side. When Barney would pet one of the other dogs, Seegoo would reach up with his paw for some attention. While Barney was busy getting acquainted with his team, Uncle Charlie disappeared for a moment around the corner of the shed and came back pushing a beautiful sled in front of him.

Barney rushed over.

"Oh, Uncle Charlie, is that for me too?"

"A team's no good without a sled, Barney," Uncle Charlie answered. "Sled dogs aren't just pets up here. They're used for working. I'll expect you to go for ice and on trips for me once in a while."

"You bet I will." Barney was sure that driving his dogs and his shiny new sled was one job he wouldn't mind. Now *he* could take Anagik for a ride and he would have his own team to go prospecting.

Uncle Charlie showed him how to harness and hitch his dogs. First the sled was braced behind a post so the dogs couldn't run away with it. Then a long towline was laid out on the ground and fastened to the front of the sled.

"Now, Barney, attach Seegoo's harness to the front of the towline so he can hold it straight while you hitch the rest of your team," Uncle Charlie directed. "Remember you always hitch your leader first. He gets his water and food first too."

"What do I feed them?" Barney asked. He was certainly going to take the best care of his dog team.

"They get a dried salmon and a bucket of water at the end of a day," Uncle Charlie answered. By now, Seegoo was hitched. Then, Uncle Charlie showed Barney how to put harnesses on the other two dogs. They were so anxious to get going it was all Barney could do to hold them. They tugged and pulled and rolled around in the snow and seemed to be having a fine time.

"They love to hit the trail," Uncle Charlie said. "No matter how hard they work, they're always anxious to go next time."

It's a good thing the sled's braced behind the post, Barney decided as he fastened the dogs to the towline. All of them were barking wildly and straining at their harnesses to be on the way.

"Now, for your first lesson in dog team driving," Uncle Charlie said as he stepped on the runners at the back of the sled. "Suppose you sit in the sled and watch me work the dogs down to the river. It's safe for travel now and an easier way to Anagik's than through the village."

Uncle Charlie grabbed the sled handle and eased the sled around the post, then he gave a shout.

"All right!" and the dogs were off like a flash.

At the village square, Uncle Charlie called, "Haw, haw, Seegoo, haw." Seegoo almost stopped, then turned and started left.

When they reached the front door of the Trading Post, Uncle Charlie gave the command, "Whoa!" and stamped on an iron claw brake between the runners at the back of the sled.

Seegoo stopped perfectly still.

"Seegoo's a good leader, Barney. Now I'll let you take over. Remember you call "gee" to go right, and "haw" to go left. The one thing you have to be very careful of is meeting other dog teams. Try and give them as wide a berth as possible or else they'll tangle and fight and there's no separating them. Sled dogs fight to the death. Remember that."

Uncle Charlie stepped off the runners. "Well, she's all yours. There's no speed limit up here. The only rule in dog sled driving is to be alert. The dogs are well trained. You won't find it hard to handle them."

Barney took his place at the back of the sled. He put his hands firmly on the sled handle and one foot down hard on the brake. Seegoo was looking back at him waiting for the command to go.

"All right!" Barney yelled, taking his foot off the brake.

Seegoo leaped forward and they were on their way skimming across the snow, down the river bank on to the smooth ice of the river. Barney knew they weren't going nearly so fast as he'd ridden in a car but it seemed much faster with the cold air hitting his face and the sled rocking from side to side as they sped along. Barney saw Anagik's cabin on the left.

"Haw!" he shouted and jerked the sled around.

Seegoo trotted up the river bank and stopped the moment Barney called "whoa" in front of Anagik's.

Anagik came running out.

"Barney! Where'd you get the team?"

"They're mine, Anagik," Barney said proudly. "Now we can go prospecting for sure!"

"Gee, that's right, we can." Anagik stood back admiring Barney's three, matched white dogs. "They're certainly beauties."

"I've come to take you on a dog sled trip," Barney said. Anagik looked at Barney and they both laughed.

"We never thought you'd be taking me, did we?" Anagik exclaimed. "Where're you going, Barney?"

Barney was stumped. He really didn't know any place to go.

"Anywhere you say."

"Well, Mother needs some firewood. We might go down the beach and bring back a load for her," Anagik suggested as he climbed into the sled.

"OK," Barney let his foot off the iron claw brake. "All right, Seegoo!" All the dogs started out with as much pep as if they'd just been hitched.

"Don't go over any snow on the river," Anagik warned, "the ice may be thin underneath."

Barney directed the team down to the river. As they whizzed along, dogs chained to posts by the river bank barked madly. Seegoo and the team kept going straight ahead, down to the river mouth and south along the beach.

"Do you think they'll be well enough trained to take us prospecting?"

"Oh, sure. You've a swell team, Barney. Look how they all work together and how they're all trotting at an easy pace. They can go all day like that."

Barney and Anagik took turns driving. Anagik showed Barney how to help the dogs along with a skipping push of the foot and by talking to them. He would clap his hands and give a shout to make them speed up.

Barney decided dog sledding was more fun than anything he'd ever done. He liked riding in the sled but best of all he liked driving the dogs. He enjoyed talking to them. When Seegoo looked back at his master, Barney would encourage him.

"Attaboy, Seegoo, nice going." Then Seegoo's ears would stand straight and his tail would curl up in the air and he would pull harder than ever.

They stopped in a little while and gathered a load of driftwood for Anagik's mother. It was Anagik's turn to drive, so Barney perched on the pile of wood in the sled when they started back.

"This makes a heavy load for the dogs," Anagik said helping them along with a push.

"Maybe someday, they'll have to pull a sled just as heavy only it'll be loaded with gold," Barney said dreamily.

"Gee, I sure wish spring would hurry and come. I know of a little marsh where no one else has been. I discovered it hunting snow shoe rabbits last year. We might look there."

Barney wanted to hear all about it—what they should take, how to get there, how long they would stay. He and Anagik were so busy talking it seemed the village was in sight in no time at all.

Suddenly, Anagik interrupted, "There's Achebuk." He pointed to a figure up on the bank gathering driftwood. Barney turned to look.

Just as he did, the dogs gave a lunge forward and broke into a gallop. There was a shout. Anagik had been thrown from the back of the sled! Barney looked forward. Ahead about a quarter of a mile was another dog team. Seegoo was going full speed for it. Barney clung to the rim of the sled as it slid and bounced along and thought of Uncle Charlie's warning: "Sled dogs fight to the death."

Behind him, he could hear Anagik yelling but the dogs were barking so furiously, he couldn't make out any words.

I have to stop my dogs, Barney said to himself. He climbed over the side of the sled until he was standing on the runners. Then he worked his way around to the back inch by inch. It was very dangerous. The sled with its load of wood might turn over at any moment but Barney didn't stop to think of that.

At last he could jump on the brake with both feet.

"Whoa!" he screamed as loudly as he could. Seegoo

slowed down and looked around as if asking if Barney really meant to spoil the fun.

"Whoa!" Barney said again, very firmly. Seegoo stopped. Barney gave a deep sigh of relief. Then he walked up to his leader and stroked the dog.

"Good boy, Seegoo, good boy." Seegoo looked up at Barney and wagged his tail.

As soon as Barney got his breath, he started back for Anagik. Both Anagik and Achebuk were waiting.

"Nice going," Anagik told Barney as he drew up and stopped the team. "I thought you were going to lose your dogs in a fight."

Achebuk stood looking solemnly at Barney. Then all at once, he grinned broadly and held out his hand.

"You drive dogs good, like Eskimo," he said.

Barney grasped Achebuk's hand firmly with his. "Thanks."

"He's already discovered gold, too!" Anagik broke in. Then he told Achebuk how Barney had found gold in the duck gizzard.

"We're going prospecting after break-up," Barney added.

Achebuk shook his head and laughed. "You hunt gold," he said, "I hunt seal."

"I just hope we turn out to be as good hunters as you are, Achebuk," Anagik answered.

"I hope so too," Barney declared firmly, for wasn't Achebuk the best hunter in the village and didn't he always bring back what he went after?

7

STORMY PLACE

Every day after school, Barney took his dog team out for a run or to get ice for Uncle Charlie. Each time it seemed they followed his commands better. Seegoo could now go straight to the front door of the Trading Post from anywhere Barney happened to give the order "Go home." They would certainly be in shape to go prospecting when break-up came and Barney was a Sourdough.

Every Saturday, Barney worked at the Trading Post.

All in all, he was so busy it didn't seem possible the day he took home his first report card from Unalakleet school that he'd been living with Uncle Charlie six weeks.

Report card day turned out to be an exciting time.

The first blizzard of the winter came to Unalakleet. It started just before lunch with sharp gusts of north wind. The weather turned very cold during the afternoon and swirling snow began to fill the air. By the time school was out, the snow was so thick Barney could hardly make out the Trading Post across the square.

Older students all waited for their little sisters and brothers when classes were over. Several mothers came for their children to make sure they wouldn't lose their way. Miss Royluk and the Fishers told everyone to go straight home. Then they started out with the smaller pupils whose families didn't come to meet them.

Barney watched all the preparations. He didn't want to leave. He wanted to stay and work on the book ends he was making for his Dad's Christmas present. With no one else using the tools, he could get a lot more done than in regular class. Anyway, I'll just stay for a little while and the storm will probably die down by the time I'm ready to go, Barney argued to himself as he went downstairs to the manual arts room.

He set to work sanding and putting a coat of varnish on the bookends. He had just finished cleaning his brushes when a blast of wind hit the building broadside. It seemed as if the walls would almost give way.

The storm must be getting worse, Barney thought with a start. He'd been so busy, he hadn't noticed. He put on his parka and ran upstairs. When he looked out he saw the storm *was* much worse!

I'd better get to the Post in a hurry, Barney decided, opening the outer door. The wind and snow hit him so hard, it made him catch his breath. The snow blew in his eyes and stung his face. It was so dark, Barney couldn't see the steps. He felt his way down and started across the square walking backwards. He felt as if the churning snow were smothering him.

Barney walked for several minutes. All at once, he realized he should have reached the Trading Post but he hadn't. Worse than that, he had no idea exactly where he was—whether he'd passed the Post or whether it was still ahead. He might not even be near the big building.

Barney turned around and faced the gale. He held his arm up to protect his eyes but still couldn't see anything. He knew it was useless to call out. The howling wind would drown his voice.

Barney was frightened. He didn't know what to do. He wished he'd gone home after school with the rest of the children when it was still light. Why had he been so foolish?

Barney was not only frightened, he was cold. He began to shake from head to toe.

Well I've got to keep going or I'll freeze, he told himself and started on again. He knew the Trading Post was in the same direction from where the wind was blowing so he started straight into the storm. It took all of Barney's strength to push and fight his way against the wind and snow. He made slow headway.

Suddenly he stumbled and fell against something. The "something" moved and let out a joyous bark. Barney would know that bark anywhere. It was Seegoo, jumping all over him, licking his face and hands, begging to be petted.

"Good old Seegoo," Barney said out loud, giving his leader a hardy thump on the side, then he stopped short. He'd walked all the way past the Trading Post and was nearly to the river bank. "You're going to take me to the Trading Post, Fellow."

He unchained Seegoo. "Go home!"

The wind blew harder than ever. Seegoo's ears went down, he tucked his tail between his legs but he drove straight ahead. In just a few moments, Seegoo stopped at the front door of the Trading Post.

Barney felt for the door knob and stepped inside stamping and beating the snow off his boots and parka. "Is that you, Barney?" Uncle Charlie came hurrying down the stairs.

"Yes, Sir," Barney yelled back. My! the fire in the big iron stove felt good! It was certainly nice to be in out of the storm.

"You gave me a scare, Boy. Where've you been?"

Barney told Uncle Charlie how he'd stayed late after school and when he'd finally started to the Post it was so dark and the snow blowing so hard he'd lost his way. Then he went on to tell of Seegoo bringing him to the front door.

"Is it all right if Seegoo stays inside tonight, Uncle Charlie?" he asked.

"It sure is. You can chain him right here beside the door," Uncle Charlie answered. "Well, Barney, I guess you found out this afternoon what the name 'Unalakleet' means."

"What's that?" Barney gave Seegoo a final pat for the night.

"Why, Unalakleet is an Eskimo word meaning 'stormy place.'"

"Then I'd say it's well named," Barney said as they started upstairs.

"We'll be having guests tonight, Barney."

Barney stopped with one foot in the air.

"We will! Who?"

"An airplane pilot and an old friend of mine who's done a lot of prospecting around here." They went into the front room. "Barney, I want you to meet Slim Dickson. We've hit a lot of trails together and been partners in prospecting on and off since the days of 1898."

Barney shook hands with a man about as old as Uncle Charlie. He had a brown leathery face and smoked a pipe.

"And this is Johnny Quinn," Uncle Charlie continued, "one of the best bush pilots in Alaska."

Johnny was a tall young man with a nice smile and wavy yellow hair.

"What kind of a pilot did Uncle Charlie say you were?" Barney asked as they shook hands.

"Bush pilot," Johnny smiled, "that means I fly in

the bush—out in the wilds where there aren't many landing fields."

"What do you do?"

"Oh," Johnny shrugged his shoulders, "you do the best you can, land on a lake or sand spit or on the tundra."

Just then a big gust of wind hit so hard, it shook the building and made the windows rattle.

"This is about the worst blizzard I've seen since '34," Slim said rubbing his hands together in front of the stove. "Remember that one, Charlie? That was the time Shahlik tried to come home from reindeer herding. The storm was so bad he couldn't see, so he finally gave up and pitched camp. When it was over, he found he'd been right outside the village the whole time and didn't know it."

Uncle Charlie laughed and nodded.

"Yep, I remember. That was the winter it was so cold, no thermometer hereabouts could go far enough below zero to record it."

Velik came to the entrance and announced supper.

I'm not going to mind this blizzard at all, Barney thought as they all went into the kitchen. Not with such interesting company.

While they were eating, Slim told of his prospecting.

"Charlie, you remember that claim I staked inland from the hot springs about eleven years ago?"

Uncle Charlie nodded.

"Well, the first clean-up I took over $3,000 out of my sluice box."

"You did!"

"Sure did. Then the second clean-up not near so much. By the third one, she was entirely worked out. That's the trouble. I've hit pay dirt several times but it never holds out."

There was a pause. It was a good chance for Barney to ask a question.

"What's a clean-up, Uncle Charlie?"

"Why, that's when you empty the gold out of your sluice box."

Barney was still puzzled.

"Sluice box?"

"A sluice box is like a small sliding board with cross pieces," Uncle Charlie explained. "You shovel dirt onto it, then wash it down with water. The gold stays on the bottom because it's heavier and is caught by the little cross pieces."

"Will I get to work a sluice box when I go prospecting?" Barney wanted to know. It sounded as if it would be fun.

"Well, that depends. First you pan in the creek beds to see if there's any gold around."

"Like this." Slim jumped up and grabbed a pan off the wash stand. He knelt down and gently rocked the pan in a whirling motion. "The dirt spills off with the water and the gold goes to the bottom—if there is any."

Just then, Seegoo started barking.

"I'll go see what the matter is," Barney excused himself and went downstairs. Seegoo jumped up and barked and wagged his tail when he saw his master. There didn't seem to be anything wrong.

"What's the matter, Seegoo? Were you lonesome?"

Right at that moment, Barney heard a pounding on the front door. So that was what Seegoo had been trying to tell him! He hurried to the door and pulled it open.

An Eskimo woman stumbled in out of the blizzard.

"Traeger here?" she asked shaking the snow from her parka. She looked very worried.

"Yes, he is," Barney invited her to follow him upstairs.

"Why, hello, Miowak, what brings you out on a night like this?" Uncle Charlie asked rising to meet her. "Is something wrong?"

The woman nodded.

"Ongan not come home. Dog team come back. Broken towline. No sled. No Ongan. Two sons with him."

Uncle Charlie's face grew serious.

"You mean the dogs broke their towline and left Ongan and your two sons out in this storm?"

Miowak nodded.

"Where did Ongan go? Do you know how far away they are?" Uncle Charlie asked.

"Ongan go toward Yukon two days away. Dogs tired, hungry."

Johnny Quinn came up, "What's the matter?"

"Something serious, John," Uncle Charlie told him. "Ongan and his two boys are stranded sixty miles inland in this blizzard. We could look for them by dog team when the storm's over but all signs of their trail would be covered and they'd be pretty hard to find."

Johnny listened closely, then he walked over to Miowak, "I'll go look for them," he promised, "just as soon as the wind dies down and it's light."

Miowak clasped her hands together, "Kooyahnah (thank you) Kooyahnah (thank you)," she said.

"I'll need somebody to lend a hand digging my plane out of the snow and it'd be a good idea if someone flew with me and helped look," Johnny told Uncle Charlie.

Barney looked up. Oh how he'd like to go along on the rescue trip!

"Well," Uncle Charlie said. "Well. . . ."

Barney dug his hands deep into his pockets and bit his lip, he was hoping so hard Uncle Charlie would think of him.

"I don't think I could leave the Post," Uncle Charlie paused, "Slim would probably go with you—but he can't see well enough to be of much help," Uncle Charlie rubbed his chin, "Paneok's been sick with a cold for two days, Tagiak can't leave the post office. How about Barney here?"

"Barney?" Johnny looked pleased, "he'd be just fine. I have to be careful not to overload my plane anyway. How about it, Barney, what do you say?"

Barney felt like jumping up and down but he tried not to show how anxious he was to go. He was still afraid Uncle Charlie might think he was too young.

"I'll be glad to go along and help in any way I can," he told Johnny man to man.

"Good," the bush pilot nodded, "then I'll tell you what we'd better do. We'd better turn in right away because the minute the storm dies down, we'll start digging out the plane so we can leave when it's light."

Barney was disappointed. He would like to have stayed up and heard some more about prospecting from Slim and of Johnny's adventures flying. Then he realized that lives were at stake. It was no time to think of what he would like to do instead of what he should. Perhaps this experience of Johnny's would be one of the most exciting yet and Barney would share it!

"OK," he said cheerfully. "Goodnight everyone."

"I stay by window and watch for wind to stop," Miowak said.

"Now, Miowak, you'd better try and get some sleep. I'll watch for the storm to pass," Uncle Charlie offered.

"Miowak no sleep tonight," Miowak shook her head. She walked over to the window and looked out into the wild night.

Barney felt very sorry for her. He hoped for all he was worth he could help Johnny find her family. "But the best way to help now is to get some sleep" he told himself walking into his room. He undressed quickly and crawled into bed.

The next thing Barney knew, Johnny was shaking him by the shoulder, "Come on, Barney. The wind's died down. It'll be light by the time we dig out. Let's go."

When they came outside the Post, the air was clear but so cold, each breath seemed to burn. A faint patch of grey light marked where the sun would come up.

Barney could hardly believe what he saw. It was as if he'd stepped into a different world. The village was half buried in snow drifts. Snow jammed up against all the cabins and a great, long bank, ten feet high, jutted out from the front of the Trading Post.

"Come on, there's no time to waste." It was Johnny.

Barney took one more look at the magic the blizzard had left and ran toward the pilot.

They found the plane surrounded by snow three feet deep. Johnny gave a long whistle. "That'll take a lot of digging," he said, handing Barney one of the two shovels he was carrying.

As it grew light, several boys Barney knew at school came down to see what was going on. When they found

out that Barney and Johnny were going to look for
Ongan, they brought shovels and helped too. It wasn't
very long until the plane was free. Barney was surprised to see it had skis instead of wheels. Just as he
and Johnny laid down their shovels, Miowak came up
pushing a sled with a tin of gasoline on it. "For you,"
she said to Johnny.

"You shouldn't have bought this, Miowak," Johnny
exclaimed.

"Village buy it," she said. "Everybody help."

Johnny quickly emptied the tin into his tank, then
putting one foot on the wing of the plane, hoisted himself up. Barney followed.

Johnny gunned the motor several times rocking the
plane to shake the frozen skis loose. Some of the
Eskimos helped by pushing. Barney felt the plane start
forward. He turned and waved good-bye as they
skimmed down the frozen river and took off.

In the village below everything was white except the
dark patches of cabin roofs.

"I'm heading toward the Yukon," Johnny said.
"We'll follow the trail Miowak says they usually took.
Unless they've had an accident, they'll be walking—
probably on a frozen stream."

Barney tried to look over every foot of land. Before long Johnny spoke again:

"We're coming to the mountains, so keep a sharp eye out. I'll look ahead and you watch directly below for any sign of something moving."

Johnny twisted the plane over a winding creek bed through a mountain pass. Once or twice, Barney thought he saw someone but it just turned out to be logs or rocks.

"It's beginning to look bad," Johnny said after awhile, "maybe we'd better turn back and—"

Before he could finish, Barney broke in,

"No, wait. I think I see someone!" he said excitedly.

"Where?" Johnny leaned forward.

"Just ahead on the right!" Barney squinted his eyes and looked harder. Yes! it was a man sure enough—running to the center of the creek bed waving his arms. Two other figures came out from the trees.

"There they are! Good boy, Barney!" Johnny dived over the waving figures to let them know they'd been seen, then he climbed again, "Now to set this plane down. We just passed a frozen lake that looked good."

He started the plane back and circled over the lake.

"Yep," he said, "we won't have any trouble landing."

Barney looked at the flat, white round place. It looked terribly small for a landing field. Trees began to come closer. Barney shut his eyes as he saw them almost brush against the plane. When he opened them, the plane was taxiing to a stop and Miowak's husband was running toward them waving his arms.

Johnny pushed the door open, "Everyone safe?"

Ongan began shouting. "Glad you come, glad you come. Dogs run away. Bad storm—"

"Yes, we know," Johnny jumped out of the plane and shook hands with Ongan. "Say, your face is frost-bitten." The skin on the Eskimo's cheeks, chin and forehead was white as snow.

"We have accident," Ongan explained as his two sons came up. One of them was limping, "His foot frozen," he added.

"Then, we'd better get you back right away," Johnny said. He and Barney helped the three trappers into the plane and a few minutes later they were in the air on their way back to Unalakleet.

During the trip, Ongan told how he and his sons had been going up the creek bed when their sled and all supplies went through the ice.

"Spring in river make water warm, ice thin," he said.

The sharp ice had broken the towline and his dogs had run away. After that, Ongan and his sons started walking toward the village and then they were caught in the blizzard. They'd made a shelter out of branches to keep warm through the night and had started out again when morning came. Today had been bad for they were tired and hungry and it was very cold.

"Maybe not get home if you not come," Ongan finished.

"I'm glad I could," Johnny said.

"Me too," Barney echoed.

Back at the village, a big crowd was out to meet them. Uncle Charlie was there and Reverend Lindgren and the nurse with her little black bag. A dog sled was waiting to take Ongan and his sons home.

When the door of the plane was opened, the nurse rushed up and everyone in the crowd craned forward. There was a low murmur of relief as Barney and Johnny helped Ongan and his sons out. Miowak stepped out from the others and went up to her husband. Barney was surprised there was no hugging or kissing.

Ongan said something to her in Eskimo. She nodded and looked down at the ground. Then waving the dog sled driver aside, Ongan turned and started for home.

Miowak came over to Barney and Johnny. Her eyes were full of tears. She feels just as much as anybody else, only she doesn't show it, Barney thought.

"You save my husband and sons," she said to Johnny. Then she turned to Barney, "You save them too. I never forget. From now on, my home, your home. You be son like my own."

Barney swallowed hard to keep the tears out of his own eyes. Miowak was adopting him into her family. From now on, Barney had an Eskimo foster mother.

8

CHRISTMAS AT UNALAKLEET

"I see it, Anagik! I see the one!" Barney yelled excitedly, stomping his foot on the sled brake and calling to Seegoo to whoa.

"Where?" Anagik raised up on his knees in the sled to look.

"Over there about half way up the hill," Barney pointed to his right. "It's perfectly shaped and just the right size. That'll make a swell Christmas tree!"

"You're right," Anagik agreed. "It's the one we need."

"Then let's go get her," Barney shouted. "Come on, Seegoo, gee, gee!" Seegoo and the rest of the team started off with a leap. They were enjoying the holidays as much as their young master and his friend.

It was the day before Christmas and Barney and Anagik were getting a Christmas tree for the party Uncle Charlie was giving that night.

"We'd better hurry or we'll never get home before dark," Barney said slowing the dogs to a stop and tying Seegoo to a small spruce tree.

It was only one thirty in the afternoon but already the sun was getting low.

Anagik picked up the ax they'd brought along and started chopping. It wasn't long before the Christmas tree was down and on the sled.

"Looks like it's going to be dark before we get home," Barney said worriedly to Anagik. "Can we make it?"

"Sure," Anagik told him, "I know a short cut. Let's take that. It'll be up and down hill a lot more but we'll get home quicker."

"OK," Barney agreed, "you drive, since you know the way."

Anagik took his place on the runners and they started on the short cut—straight up hill. It was a hard pull for the dogs. Barney got out of the sled and helped Anagik push. When they came to the top, they stopped for a minute to rest. They were up so high, they could see the country for several miles around.

Suddenly Barney stopped and stared.

"Anagik," he whispered, "there's some kind of animal on that far hill. Look—over there."

Anagik laughed when he saw what Barney was pointing out.

"Those are reindeer, Barney. They're usually farther inland this time of year."

Reindeer! Barney grabbed Uncle Charlie's field glasses out of their case and took a close look. The reindeer were just a little smaller than cows and had white and brown coats. They had horns too, just like those Barney had seen in the picture of his "Night Before Christmas" book when he was a little boy.

Barney laughed.

"Well, I should have known there would be reindeer around this close to Santa Claus land, or do the kids up here know about Santa Claus?"

"They're beginning to," Anagik told him, "but when I was little, we never had Santa Claus, Christmas trees or anything like that."

"Well, this year, you're going to have a tree, Anagik, because you're invited to Uncle Charlie's Christmas party. You're coming, aren't you?"

"Sure," Anagik replied, "but we'd better get going or we'll never get back in time."

Barney looked at his wrist watch.

"You're right. It's almost three o'clock."

"Gee, that's a nice watch, Barney, when'd you get that?"

"Bought it with money I earned on my paper route back home," Barney told him; "it keeps good time too."

"It's a beauty. Some day when I get to be a trapper, I'll earn enough to have one for myself."

They reached the top of another hill and started down. The sled was going very fast. Anagik clamped his foot hard on the brake. With a warning shout, he swerved sharply to miss a big rock. Barney felt the sled going over and started to brace himself. Before he could catch hold, there was another lurch and Barney sailed head first into the snow along with the Christmas tree.

Anagik came running back as Barney jumped up and shook the snow off his parka.

"Are you OK?"

"Sure," Barney answered helping Anagik lift the tree on the sled and climbing aboard himself.

Anagik cut over to the regular trail which wound through woods at the base of the hills. They jogged along for some time. By now, it was completely dark. Finally Anagik spoke.

"It won't be long, Barney. We'll come into the open just around this hill, then it's only a mile and a half."

As the sled came out of the forest, Barney caught his breath at what he saw. The whole sky ahead of them was ablaze with pink, green, yellow and blue northern lights. All shades of colored streamers floated through the air. They were so bright, they even gave the snow a pinkish hue. Anagik stopped the sled so they could enjoy the sight.

"If you whistle, they'll come closer," he told Barney, then he whistled. Almost at once, it *did* seem, one of the streamers dipped toward them. Barney tried, too, but his whistling didn't make much difference.

"They are bright tonight!" Anagik said.

"They sure are," Barney agreed climbing back into the sled. "There, for a minute, I thought that spill I took on my head had me seeing things!" He watched the display as Anagik drove the dogs. "With some-thing as nice as the northern lights on Christmas Eve, you don't need any Christmas tree."

By the time they reached the Trading Post, there were just two hours left before the party. They all had to hurry to get the tree trimmed. Velik made a base for it. Barney and Anagik put on the bright glass balls and tinsel. Finished and standing in one corner of the front room, it was the prettiest tree Barney had ever seen. He hurried to put the presents he'd bought for everyone underneath and since there was no one watching, he picked up the box that had come from Porterville on last Friday's plane and shook it. Then Barney couldn't help laughing. Fran was prob-ably doing exactly what he'd just done—poking around the gifts under the Christmas tree at home! Well, she'd never guess from the way he'd packed it that her present was a little doll bed he'd made. And Mother and Dad would be surprised to find nicely carved book ends and a lamp in their packages. Later on, they would all gather around the piano and sing Christmas carols.

Barney began to feel a little homesick. Just then, there was a knock at the door. The guests began to

arrive and there was no more time for thoughts of home.

His foster mother, Miowak and her husband, the man he and Johnny had rescued after the blizzard, came in. Achebuk, who had seen Barney almost go through the ice and directed him to safety, was next to arrive and Uncle Charlie's Eskimo cook, Velik, stayed on after dinner. Of course, Anagik was there too.

The party was lots of fun. Everyone laughed and talked. Velik told stories of some of the old medicine men who used to live in the village. Uncle Charlie brought out home made ice cream, cookies, nuts and coffee. Barney never thought he'd be eating ice cream with the Eskimos, but he was and it tasted good. What's more, they liked it just as much as he did.

Barney liked the stories and the refreshments but he could hardly wait for the time they would open gifts.

At last Uncle Charlie walked over to the tree.

"Well, well, it looks like Santa Claus has been here! Shall we see what he's brought?"

The Eskimos all laughed and grinned.

"Yes, let's!" Barney was so anxious, he shouted.

They all gathered around the tree. Uncle Charlie handed out gifts to the guests first. With the money Barney earned working at the Trading Post, he'd bought a scarf for each of the women and a pair of warm wool socks for the men. Everyone was very pleased with the presents and thanked Barney over and over. Next came Barney's gift to Uncle Charlie. It was a footstool he'd made in manual arts at school. Uncle Charlie took it right over to his big chair and tried it out while everyone watched and laughed.

Barney couldn't wait any longer.

"You haven't given Anagik his present yet," he blurted out.

"Why, I guess you're right, Barney. Let's see now, what did Santa leave for Anagik?"

Uncle Charlie dug out a tiny package, much smaller than any of the others.

"Here you are, Anagik. I guess you've been a good boy after all!"

Anagik took the present. He shook it and smelled it trying to guess what it was but finally gave up. When he opened it and saw what it was, he was so surprised he almost dropped it. It was Barney's wrist watch!

"Barney, you shouldn't have done it. Gee, it's beautiful. I can't believe it's mine—" Anagik showed it to the rest of the Eskimos. They all crowded around and oh'd and ah'd.

"Here, here," Uncle Charlie interrupted. "Looks like someone else has been a good boy," and he began giving Barney his presents. The package from Porterville contained a red sweater knit by Mother. Dad sent a down sleeping bag. Now how did he know this is just what I need for prospecting, Barney wondered, trying the zipper. And Fran must have robbed her pig bank to buy the waterproof box for matches.

There never was such a Christmas as this one for Barney!

Miowak had made him a beautiful pair of waterproof seal skin trousers. "For when you go out on trail," she explained.

Achebuk went over behind the door in the kitchen and brought out an ice pick he'd hidden when he came in. "So you know when ice is safe," he said and grinned.

There was a good looking pair of snow shoes Velik had made and on top of all these things, Uncle Charlie gave Barney a rifle.

"That's for when you go out on trail—prospecting," Uncle Charlie told him.

The last thing Barney picked up was his present from Anagik. It was small—as his own gift to Anagik had been. He couldn't imagine what it was. It felt light and when he shook it, there was no rattle. Barney tore off the wrapping. It was a bracelet.

"It's made of old ivory my father found on the beach long ago," Anagik told him.

On three of the links, Anagik had carved a dog, on a fourth link, a sled, and on the last one a figure of a boy driving a dog team. It was Barney driving his team! Barney knew Anagik had spent a lot of time making such a fine bracelet.

"It's a beauty, Anagik. How do I fasten it on?"

Anagik looked at Barney, then he looked at the floor. Barney could see something was wrong,

"What's the matter, Anagik? It *is* a bracelet, isn't it?"

"Yes, it's a bracelet," Anagik said. There was a pause. Everyone waited for him to go on. "Only it's a bracelet for your watch," he finished.

"For my watch!" Barney exclaimed, "that's swe—" Then he stopped short. He didn't *have* a watch. He'd given his watch to Anagik. They looked at each other and began to laugh. What a good joke! Barney had a watch bracelet and no watch. Anagik had a watch and he'd just given away a beautiful ivory watchband.

"Well, well," Uncle Charlie broke in. "Barney will have to tell time by the sun and Anagik will have to be satisfied with an ordinary watch strap instead of a carved ivory one. Those are mighty fine gifts and I'd say you're both real lucky."

"I'd say," Barney echoed, "not any of the fellows I know in Porterville have a watch band like this or any of the wonderful gifts you've all given me," he added turning to the rest of the guests. "This has been one of the nicest Christmases I've ever had."

"Me too," Anagik said. "Whenever I look at the time I'll remember this Christmas. I'm going to lend the watch to my Father when he times the dog races on New Year's Day."

New Year's Day! The day when there would be all sorts of games and contests. It was at the New Year's Day celebrations that Mayuk's Father had beaten Anagik's Father a long time ago. Now this year, their two sons would kick against each other. It would be a thrilling contest for every one knew how both Ana-

gik and Mayuk wanted to win. Barney had been practicing hard and now he could kick almost as high as
Anagik.

A week seemed awfully long but with doing chores
for Uncle Charlie and taking Seegoo and the dogs
out, the holidays went by in a hurry. In no time at
all, Barney was standing in the square with all the
villagers watching the New Year's Day dog team races.
As he watched he thought how much fun it would be
to have his own team in the races but he knew his
dogs wouldn't have a chance against some of the big
teams with eleven dogs. The teams had to go six miles
out of the village and back. They left one at a time.
Anagik's Father kept time on each of them with Barney's Christmas watch. The first team was given five
minutes to break trail. While they were out, there were
snowshoe races for both the men and women.

They were hardly finished before some of the villagers standing on the big snow bank in front of the
Trading Post started yelling, "Dog teams coming! Dog
teams coming!"

"Come on, let's see who it is." Anagik ran toward
the mission where his Father was keeping time. Everyone was excited, running back and forth shouting and

wanting "their" team to come in first. By late afternoon, all the teams were in and the winner decided.
It was Tagiak, the Postmaster. His team of nine white
dogs did the twelve miles in a little over 46 minutes.

Now the crowd went inside the school house for
the finger pull and the long-looked-for double kick.

Twenty-two boys besides Mayuk, Anagik and Barney entered the double kick. It started with the ball
hung about three and a half feet off the ground. This
was easy for Barney and Anagik. In their practice,
they'd kicked shoulder high but about a third of the
boys dropped out. Mayuk was still in, however, and
had no trouble at all touching the ball.

The Eskimos looked surprised when they saw Barney enter the contest. They didn't have any idea he
knew how to double kick. Barney was glad he'd done
some faithful practicing.

On the next round, the ball went up a foot. This
was about as high as Barney had ever kicked. Many
of the boys couldn't come near the ball. When the
round ended, only Barney, Mayuk, Anagik and two
others were in.

The ball went up three inches. The two boys whose
names Barney didn't know tried first. One of them

couldn't touch the ball at all. The other just barely touched it with one foot but that wasn't enough so they were both out. Then, Mayuk stepped in front of the ball. He turned around and smiled calmly at the crowd. Anagik nudged Barney.

"Mayuk thinks he's won the double kick already."

Mayuk stood there a few moments studying the height of the ball, then, taking a deep breath, he ran a few short steps and kicked.

The ball moved! Mayuk had touched the ball at 4′ 9″. Some of the crowd started arguing. Had he touched it with both feet? Everyone talked excitedly. One of the judges came forward and raised his arm for silence.

"Mayuk did *not* touch the ball with both feet. He is out."

Anagik gripped Barney's arm.

"You've got to touch it, Barney. If you don't and I don't, it'll be a tie."

Barney stepped into the ring. Everybody stopped talking and watched. He took several deep breaths, then with doubled fists ran a few steps and kicked so hard, he thought his back would break. There was a shout.

Anagik rushed up. "You did it, Barney. You touched the ball with both feet. Mayuk is beaten."

Barney couldn't help grinning, he felt so good. Then he remembered. Anagik was still in. They had to kick against each other! Anagik must have been thinking the same thing, for his face became very sober. Barney was first to speak.

"It doesn't matter, Anagik, if you win or I win. The big thing was to beat Mayuk and we both wanted that."

Anagik stepped forward. He looked at the ball, grinned at Barney and kicked. He touched it! Now it was between these two friends. Everyone watched very closely as the ball was raised three more inches. Barney stepped up. This was the real test. He bent his knees to loosen up, ran a few steps, straightened up, and kicked almost in the same movement. There was a low murmur from the crowd. He had barely touched the ball with his right foot but had missed it entirely with his left.

"Too bad, Barney," Anagik said as he came up to try.

Anagik measured the height of the ball, stepped back and stood relaxed for a second. Then taking his place he ran a few swift steps and with a mighty leap and kick his feet went above his head to hit the ball. Everyone shouted. Anagik was the winner and no doubt about it. Barney was the first to reach him and shake hands.

"Nice going, Anagik, I'm glad you won."

That night after dinner Barney told Uncle Charlie all about the games and the double kick contest.

"— so Anagik won," he finished. "I don't really know whether I wanted to win from him or not."

"And I expect Anagik felt exactly the same way," Uncle Charlie said. "That's the way with real friends."

"Yep, I guess you're right."

"That's the kind of friend to have—especially when you're prospecting. Gold sometimes makes men forget everything, even their partners, unless, of course, they're real friends." Uncle Charlie quit talking and sat thinking of his prospecting days.

Barney stood up and stretched. Jiminy! he was getting stiff.

"Think I'll turn in."

"A good idea," Uncle Charlie nodded; "you've had a pretty full week and tomorrow's Saturday you know."

Saturday! Barney's day to clerk in the Trading Post. Something interesting always happened. Barney didn't know it then but this Saturday would prove especially interesting.

9

BARNEY GOES FISHING

"Thanks very much," Barney handed a package of bright gingham to a woman customer, "that ought to make a very pretty parka covering. Who's next please?"

"Me," it was a little Eskimo girl just barely tall enough to peer over the counter.

"And what can I do for you, young lady?" Barney asked.

"I want a package of gum, please," she said holding her money out in front of her.

Barney smiled to himself as he handed her the gum. Eskimos chewing gum still seemed a little strange to him, yet all the children liked gum and candy.

"Will there be anything else?"

The little girl shook her head and ran out just as a man came through the door.

He's a trapper, Barney knew right away because he was carrying some beaver skins.

The trapper laid his skins on the counter. They had already been cleaned and stretched into a round shape.

"How much?" he asked. He meant how much would he be given in store goods for the furs.

"Just a minute," Barney hurried to get Paneok because Paneok knew enough about furs to judge their value. Trappers brought in all kinds—fox, beaver, marten, otter and, as Uncle Charlie had said, "it takes a good many years in the business to be able to know how much to pay for what."

Paneok felt how thick the fur was, he studied the pelt for any scars or holes and finally he measured it. Then he made an offer. The trapper nodded.

Meanwhile, a woman carrying her baby on her back had come in. Barney left the trapper to wait on her. She was doing her week's shopping and bought all sorts of things—canned milk, candles, dried fruits and crackers.

"Two salmon trout," she went on.

"Yes Ma'am," Barney went to the rear storage room where the frozen salmon trout were kept. Usually they were stacked in a big pile on the floor but today there wasn't a single one. When Barney came back to tell the woman he was out of salmon trout, he found her talking to an old Eskimo with white hair. It was Uncle Charlie's good friend Kootuk who supplied dried salmon for Barney's dogs. He often brought Uncle Charlie rabbits or ptarmigan he'd shot. He was a good woodsman.

"Hello, Kootuk. I'll be with you in a minute." Barney turned to the woman. "I'm sorry, we're out of salmon trout. Will there be anything else?"

She shook her head. "Nahgah."

Barney had learned by now that "nahgah" meant "no." He made out a list of everything she'd bought. These groceries would be paid for in furs her husband brought in. "It's a good thing she carries the baby on her back," he thought as he watched her leave with her arms full of groceries. Then he turned to Kootuk.

"Now, Kootuk, what will it be?"

"I hear you say no more salmon trout?" Kootuk asked.

"That's right. We've sold the last of that big pile

we had. The villagers certainly do like salmon trout."

"You want more?" Kootuk went on without waiting for an answer, "I go empty my fish trap, bring back lotsa fish."

"Just a minute, I'll ask Uncle Charlie," Barney ran upstairs. Uncle Charlie was at his desk by the window in the front room.

"Uncle Charlie, we're out of trout. Kootuk wants to know if you want any more. He says he'll go empty his fish trap if you do."

"Sure. If we need 'em. You tell Kootuk I'll give him 25¢ in store goods for every pound of fish."

"OK," Barney started to go out. Then he stopped.

"What does an Eskimo fish trap look like?" he asked.

Uncle Charlie thought a minute.

"Well, it's about two feet around and six feet long and made of wire. One end is like a funnel so the fish will go in. Say—" Uncle Charlie leaned back in his chair and pushed his glasses up on his forehead. "Would you like to SEE a real fish trap?"

"Would I? You bet I would." Barney's face lit up. Already in his mind, he was getting into his parka and heading out.

"Then I tell you what you do," Uncle Charlie went

on. "You go down and tell Kootuk I'd like him to start out to his trap this afternoon so he can be back by tomorrow night and that I said you could go with him. You'll furnish the grub and help him in any way you can."

Barney ran downstairs at full speed.

"Kootuk, Uncle Charlie says he wants to buy your fish and to go out and get them this afternoon and I can go with you and I'll bring the grub and do anything I can to help."

Kootuk's face was blank for a minute. Then he began to understand. He grinned.

"Good. I come by with dogs. You be ready."

"OK," Barney called over his shoulder. He had already started getting a box of food ready—dried fruit, potatoes, canned meat, powdered eggs, coffee, canned milk, bacon and pancake flour. Barney knew just what to take, he'd made up so many grubstakes for the trappers. Then he rushed upstairs to change into warmer clothes and get the sleeping bag Dad had sent for Christmas.

"Uncle Charlie," he called from the bedroom, "you won't forget to see that Seegoo and the team are fed and watered while I'm gone, will you?"

Uncle Charlie came to the door.

"Don't worry, I'll look after them myself. You'd better take an extra pair of wool socks. No, wait a minute, I have the very thing." He went into the front room and came back holding a pair of socks made out of rabbit skin, "Here, these'll keep your feet good and warm. Put them on now and then when you stop to camp, turn these and your boots inside out to dry."

Barney had just finished tying his boots on over the rabbit fur socks when Tagiak called up the stairs that Kootuk and his team were waiting.

"Tell him I'm coming," Barney shouted back. "Well, I guess I'm ready. Bye," he said to Uncle Charlie, "please don't forget Seegoo."

"I won't. Have a good trip and bring back lots of fish."

Barney ran down the steps, picked up the box of food and hurried outside. Kootuk had all his supplies covered with canvas and neatly roped in his sled. In the front was a stove made out of half an oil drum and on top of the load lay his rifle. Even with all Barney's things packed in there was still plenty of room.

"Go," Kootuk called to his nine dogs. They leaped

up and started out so fast, it felt to Barney as if the sled went up in the air. Down the river bank, across and almost straight up the other side. Barney jumped out to help Kootuk push the sled. It slipped and slid about while the dogs strained at their harnesses. Once up the bank, the dogs started out again full speed. Barney settled back in the sled. Working at the Post since early morning, he hadn't realized how cold it was outside. He faced half way around so the wind wouldn't hit him head on. The cold air turned Barney's breath to ice on his parka ruff.

They traveled along a trail marked with wooden tripod markers.

"This way white man went to hunt gold," Kootuk told him. So Barney was traveling over the same trail the Sourdoughs had used back in the old days. "Did any of them find gold?' he wondered to himself.

Kootuk leaned over.

"Better wipe frost off ruff," he advised, "or it freeze face quick."

Barney did as he was told.

The dogs settled into a steady lope. The trail was a narrow path of packed down snow. On either side, the snow was soft and when the sled slipped off into this, Barney would jump out to help Kootuk lift it back. It wasn't long before they went into a forest. The sun sank soon after they started but a bright three-quarter moon came up so there was enough light. Once Kootuk stopped the sled to inspect the dogs' feet. He pointed out little balls of ice like marbles between the pads on his leader's paws.

"Not good. Hurt dog," then he carefully pulled them out.

Barney didn't know what time it was but he guessed around seven o'clock when Kootuk stopped the sled beside a frozen river.

"We camp here," he said. "You take care of dogs, I put up tent."

Barney felt proud that he knew what to do. First he unhitched the leader and chained him to a small tree with one of the steel chains Kootuk had brought along. He stamped down the snow so the dog would have a comfortable place to lie, then he unharnessed and chained out the other dogs. Once this was done, he took some dried salmon out of the sled and gave one to each dog. While they were eating, Barney decided he'd better go for water. He found a bucket in the sled load and a pick—a funny old-fashioned pick

that had long, slender points. He went to where Kootuk was pounding in a tent stake.

"I'm going for ice now."

Kootuk looked up. He pointed to the pick Barney
was carrying.

"That come from white man looking for gold."

Barney felt a tingle up his spine. He was holding a
pick some prospector had used fifty years ago. Maybe
the man had even hit gold with this same pick! But
there wasn't time to stand and day dream. He hurried
down to the river to chip enough ice to fill the bucket.

By the time he was back, the tent was up.

"You empty sled, I go for wood," Kootuk told
Barney.

"OK." Barney undid the ropes holding in the sled
load. He took out the sleeping bags and put them in
the back of the tent. Then he moved in the grub and
set up the stove. Even in the tent, it was awfully cold.
Barney blew on his hands and stamped his feet to get
warm. He heard Kootuk coming and ran outside.

"I'm finished with unpacking. Now what do you
want me to do?"

Kootuk looked at Barney, then he looked at the sled
and frowned.

"Always turn sled over on side. Runners freeze to snow."

Barney hurriedly turned the sled over, then followed the old woodsman into the tent.

Kootuk frowned again.

"Need branches to lie on," he said. "You get. I cook."

Barney realized he had a lot to learn about camping.

When he came back with his arms full of branches, there was a fire going and potatoes and meat cooking on the stove. He dropped the spruce to one side and held his hands toward the stove.

"That fire feels good."

"Cottonwood make hot fire, hotter than other kinds," Kootuk told him.

Barney hated to leave the warmth but he had another job to do. He took the bucket of melted ice off the stove and went to water the dogs. When he re-entered the tent, Kootuk was heaping their tin plates with food.

"Mmmmmmmmmmm. This food tastes wonderful," Barney declared with his first bite.

"It good all right," Kootuk agreed. Then he reached over to his sleeping bag and pulled out a small package. It was dried salmon! "This good too," he said taking a bite, "better for Eskimo."

He broke off a piece for Barney. It was hard and dry.

"You like?"

Barney nodded. "But I think I have all I can eat here," he said pointing to his plate.

"It taste better with seal oil," Kootuk told him.

They ate off of the grub box with a candle in the middle for light. Right after eating, Kootuk began whittling at the end of a spruce branch. Barney watched as the Eskimo peeled the wood back into thin shavings.

"What are you making?"

"Sourdough shavings," the old man said without looking up.

"What are they used for?" Barney picked up some of the shavings from a pile by the stove. The split ends curled back like Seegoo's tail!

"To start fire quick," Kootuk explained. "Sourdough show Eskimo how to make them. Always fix night before."

When Kootuk was sure he had enough Sourdough shavings to build a fire with in the morning, he showed

Barney how to lay the rest of the spruce branches for a mattress under the sleeping bags. Then he took off his boots and tied them to the tent pole far away from the stove. Barney remembered what Uncle Charlie had told him so he turned his rabbit skin socks and boots inside out and hung them up to dry beside Kootuk's.

"Take clothes off. Dry them out too," Kootuk told him, "may be damp and freeze," he pointed to hoar frost at the corners of the tent, "Frost thick. Maybe forty below tonight."

Barney's heart turned over. He was sleeping out at forty below! In weather like this many people had frozen to death. But Barney needn't worry. He was with one of the best campers in the village. Just as soon as he was snug in his sleeping bag, Kootuk showed him how to fix the blanket over his face to keep it from freezing. Barney went to sleep as easily as if he'd been back at the Trading Post in his bed.

The next morning without even getting out of his sleeping bag, Kootuk put some shavings and wood into the stove, struck a match and within three or four minutes, the tent was warm.

Kootuk and Barney went to work on the fish trap right after breakfast.

With the river entirely frozen over, Barney had no idea where the trap was but Kootuk didn't hestitate a second. The old Eskimo went straight to the center of the frozen river where two tall poles stuck out of the ice.

"Fish trap here. Front of trap wired to poles," he said, then he began chopping with his ax behind the poles.

Barney noticed a row of posts leading off from the trap to each bank.

"What are those other posts for?" he asked.

Kootuk rested on his ax a minute.

"For fence under ice. It block river. Fish trap only place fish can go." He began chopping again. Barney helped with the prospector's pick.

"Whew!" he said after about fifteen minutes, "This ice is sure thick."

"Maybe a foot—maybe not," Kootuk kept right on chopping, "ice three feet thick when trap put in."

"You mean you chopped through three feet of ice to set this trap in?" Barney asked in amazement.

"That right," Kootuk replied.

"But why didn't you put it in before freeze-up?" Barney wanted to know.

"Trap move when ice come. No good."

"Oh," Barney started in with his prospector's pick again.

When enough ice was chipped, Kootuk would scoop it out with a shovel. Now and then, they would stop and go to the tent to get warm. Finally, after nearly two hours, all the ice was cleared away from over the trap. Kootuk took hold of the two long poles of the trap and started pulling it up on the ice,

"Ugh," he said, "heavy."

Barney came over to help. The trap was indeed heavy and for a good reason. When they finally had it out on the ice, they found it full of squirming fish!

"Gee whilakers!" Barney had never seen so many live fish all together before in his life. "How many do you figure you have there?"

"Maybe 150 pounds."

"150 pounds!" Barney echoed.

"That right," Kootuk took the back off his trap and dumped the catch out on the ice. The fish had almost all frozen stiff. "More fish than that when there's wind and storm. Make fish move in river more."

"Well, this is a good way to catch fish," Barney declared as he started putting the catch into a sack.

Kootuk was busy wiring the back to his fish trap.

"I come back in two weeks. Just as many fish," he told Barney.

When the trap was fixed, he quickly put it into the water, then he picked up two of the biggest fish in the catch.

"We eat now."

Perhaps Barney was just extra hungry from all the work but the salmon trout tasted better than any fish he'd ever eaten.

It didn't take near as long to break camp as it had to set up. While Kootuk packed the sled, Barney hitched the dogs. The minute they saw him with their harnesses, they all started barking wildly to get going.

The trip back was slow because of the extra weight of fish but with the wind behind them Barney was more comfortable riding in the sled.

"Have you ever been lost on the trail?" he asked as they whizzed along.

Kootuk thought a minute.

"Once for a little while," he said.

"How'd it happen?" Barney couldn't imagine Kootuk ever not knowing where he was.

"When I a boy—young boy. I go trap with my

Father. He take his sled ahead. I behind with my team. No trail. I follow sled tracks. Storm come up. Snow all day, all night. Cover trail up. Next day, dark sky, no sun."

"How'd you find your way back?"

"I follow snowdrifts."

"Follow snowdrifts?" Barney didn't understand.

"Wind around Unalakleet always blow from east to west. Make snowdrifts run east, west. Wind make snowdrift higher on west end. High part point toward Unalakleet."

"Well, I'd never have thought of that!"

Kootuk certainly knew a lot about life outdoors. With a trailmate like him to tell stories of hunting and trapping in the woods, it wasn't any time at all until they were back at the Trading Post and Uncle Charlie was coming through the front door.

"How was the fishing trip?"

"Fine," Barney answered starting to take his camping gear off the sled. "Kootuk says we brought back 150 pounds."

"Is that a fact!" Uncle Charlie peered under the sled cover. "I'll bet you never expected to go on a fishing trip and come back with that much fish."

"I certainly didn't," Barney agreed. "Anything happen while I was gone?" It seemed like he'd been away much longer than overnight.

"Well now, let's see. Oh yes, there was one thing. You had a visitor, your foster mother—Miowak. She wants you to come over to her house for dinner tomorrow night."

"Well swell. That ought to be fun." Barney helped Kootuk lift the sack of fish out of the sled.

"She told me she's going to have something very special for you," Uncle Charlie went on.

"What's that?" Barney stopped his unloading.

"Eskimo ice cream."

"Eskimo ice cream! Is that any different from ours?"

"It surely is!"

"What does it taste like?"

But Uncle Charlie wouldn't tell.

"You'll see," was all he would say.

10

DINNER WITH MIOWAK

Crrrrrrack! Barney drove his pick into the ice.

A big piece broke off at his feet. The ice was brittle and cracked easily in cold weather. Barney thought of the first time he'd gone for ice. Anagik went along to show him the way. Barney had been surprised when Anagik told him to go to the Bering Sea ice field.

"But won't the ice be salty here?"

"No," Anagik shook his head, "river water doesn't mix with the sea when freeze-up comes. If you're careful to stay in the river channel you can get fresh water ice out here."

"But how will I know if the ice I get is fresh water?"

Anagik took up a pick and chopped out a small piece of ice. Then he walked about ten yards away and did the same thing again. He held both pieces out to Barney.

"Fresh water ice is clear. Sea ice is milky."

Why, of course! Barney could see the difference easily.

That was several months ago. Barney had been going for ice ever since and Uncle Charlie had not yet had salty water.

Barney lifted the last chunk of today's load into the sled and jumped on the runners. "All right, Seegoo!"

With a joyful yelp, the dogs started racing across the ice. They didn't like to stay still when in harness.

An old woman was sitting all by herself at the river mouth fishing through a hole in the ice. As Barney came closer, he could see it was Kyrok, the Great Grandmother he had first met gathering wood last fall.

"Hello, Kyrok! How's fishing?"

Kyrok looked up and grinned. She and Barney had become good friends. Every time Barney came out for ice he saw her sitting there fishing. He always stopped to say a few words to her because he felt she could understand a little of what he said even if she didn't speak English. Often, there were a lot of other women fishing too. It was always the old women of the village. Fishing for tomcod seemed to be their special job.

Barney stood for a minute and watched. Fishing certainly must be good today. There was a big pile of frozen tomcod beside Kyrok. As Barney looked, the line on her short, little fishing pole jerked. With a stick she held in her right hand, Kyrok drew the line up. Sure enough! she had caught another one! She knocked the squirming tomcod off with the stick. In a few seconds she caught another. Barney was always amazed at the number of tomcod the Eskimo women could catch with just a red bead for a lure.

"Looks as if you have plenty of fish there for your family and the dogs."

Kyrok smiled as if she knew what he meant.

Barney waited until she caught three more tomcod. Usually he watched the fishing longer, but not today. He wanted get the load of ice to the Trading Post as quickly as possible so he could go over to Miowak's for dinner.

"Well, good-bye, Kyrok. All right, Seegoo!" he called, clapping his hands.

When they reached home Barney didn't waste any

time carrying the ice upstairs and dumping it into the two big barrels in the kitchen. Velik was busy cooking dinner for Uncle Charlie.

"Boy! that sure smells good, Velik."

"Want to taste?" Velik asked.

"No, sir," Barney replied firmly, "I'm saving up for some of Miowak's ice cream. Going there to dinner.

"Are you going to take your dogs?" Uncle Charlie asked, coming through the doorway.

"Nope, I think I'll walk," and walk he did. Barney had no trouble at all finding his way, the moon was so bright. The night was still and clear. It was so cold the snow creaked when he walked on it.

There was no answer when Barney knocked at the door of Miowak's cabin, so he stepped inside. Barney had found when he'd stopped by for Anagik that Eskimo cabins had an outer room. This helped keep cold air out when the main room door was opened.

Ongan must have heard the footsteps, for he opened the inside door before Barney could knock.

"Come in," he grinned and shook hands.

Miowak and her daughter stood behind him. "Yah! Yah!" (Welcome welcome!)

"Hello," Barney grinned back and stepped inside.

It was a small room. The only furniture was a little stove in one corner, a shelf and a chest against the wall. Over in another corner, lying on some reindeer skins on the floor, was one of Miowak's sons—the one whose foot had been frozen during the blizzard.

"Hello, Barney," he said, smiling.

"Hello there," Barney answered. "How's the foot?"

"Still sore from freezing but it's getting better now. Guess if it hadn't been for you, I might not be here at all."

"That right," Miowak agreed, "you save his life."

"Why, I didn't do anything anyone else wouldn't have done if they'd had the chance," Barney declared.

"No," Miowak shook her head, "you save his life and I never forget it."

Ongan sat down on the floor.

"Sit," he pointed to a place beside a low wooden platform.

Miowak set a small wooden bowl and a wooden platter with a big fish on it before Barney.

Why, this is the table! Barney realized with a start as Miowak's son and daughter sat beside him.

"Eat," Ongan said pointing to the fish. Barney didn't know exactly what to do—whether the whole fish was for him or not. Ongan settled the matter by reaching over and cutting off a piece for himself and for Barney. The fish was raw.

"This *quak*," Ongan told him. "It frozen and thawed—good as cooked," but to Barney it didn't taste quite the same.

After each bite, everyone but Barney dipped his fingers into the small wooden bowl and then licked them.

"What are you eating now?" Barney asked.

"Seal oil," Miowak told him. "Eskimo eat it with every meal."

"Old seal oil best," Ongan said.

"Oh, I see. You mean this is made from old seals."

Miowak's son laughed.

"No, Barney. What he means is that the older the seal oil is, the stronger it gets and he likes it strong. It can come from young seals as well as old. We've had this oil since last spring."

Miowak listened to her son. She rose from the table and went to the outer room. When she returned she was carrying something black. It looked a little like a queer shaped balloon.

"Put seal blubber in this. It turn to seal oil."

"What is it?" Barney looked closer and could see it was some kind of animal skin.

"Seal poke," Miowak replied, "I take insides out of seal. Empty seal skin make bag."

By now, the quak was eaten. Ongan took up some Sourdough shavings lying by the stove.

"You know what this is?" he asked.

"Sure," Barney replied proudly, "Sourdough shavings. They're used to start a fire quickly."

"Used for this, too," Ongan wiped his hands on the shavings as he would a napkin. Then he passed them around for the others.

Miowak reached over to the stove and took off a steaming pot. In it was boiled trout. Barney had no trouble eating this but he didn't dip into the seal oil between each bite as Miowak and her family did.

Next Miowak set a big wooden bowl of something white and creamy on the table. Barney could see orange, blue and red berries in it. It looked good.

"Akootuk," Ongan said in a solemn voice as if it were very fine.

Akootuk! This was the Eskimo ice cream Uncle Charlie had talked about.

Miowak's daughter looked at Barney and smiled.

"I'm glad you came. We only have akootuk once in a long while to honor a guest."

"That was very nice of you," Barney said to Miowak.

"I glad you come," Miowak answered.

Ongan dipped his fingers into the akootuk, put them in his mouth and smacked his lips.

"Nahgooruk!" he exclaimed.

Barney didn't know what that meant but he was sure from Ongan's expression that he liked the akootuk.

Barney dipped in and took a bite. The Eskimo ice cream wasn't cold, but it was creamy and soft. The berries gave it a fruity flavor.

"Say this *is* good. What's it made of?"

"It have reindeer fat—tallow you call it—and seal oil and berries," Miowak told him.

"What kind of berries?" Barney asked reaching for more.

"Salmon berries, blue berries and currants. We pick last summer. Keep in keg in cellar."

Just then, there was a knock at the door.

"Come in!" Ongan called.

The door opened and in stepped Achebuk, the man who'd helped Barney get off the river ice. He smiled at Ongan and Miowak, then he saw Barney.

"You have visitor!" he said.

"Yes." Miowak rose and motioned for Achebuk to take her place at the table. "For him, we have akootuk. You eat some too."

"Akootuk!" Achebuk's eyes opened wide. He sat down and dipped into the wooden bowl. It was easy to see he was glad he'd come. He took a big mouthful.

"Nahgooruk!" Then he turned to Barney. "You been one ice lately?" he joked.

Barney felt his ears turning red.

"I went with Kootuk to empty his fish trap yesterday," he answered.

"Good. You learn lot from Kootuk." Achebuk nodded.

Miowak came back to the table carrying a bundle of squirrel skins.

"I make parka for daughter." She held out the skins so Barney could see what tiny stitches she'd made.

"My wife best sewer in village," Ongan told Barney proudly.

Miowak smiled at her husband, then she turned to Achebuk. "How your wife?" she asked.

Achebuk's face grew sad. "Wife gone. Her Father, he sick. She go up coast to take care of him."

Ongan shook his head. "Too bad."

"Very bad," Achebuk went on, "need boots for seal hunting. No wife to sew for me."

The two men sat and stared glumly at the floor. After a while, Ongan spoke. "My wife make boots for you."

Achebuk looked up with relief. "Good," he said to Miowak, "I give you first seal I shoot."

"Too much," Miawak shook her head.

"Not too much," Achebuk insisted.

"All right," Miowak agreed. Everyone was happy again. "When you want boots for hunting?"

"Maybe two weeks," Achebuk told her. "You finish by then?"

"I finish," Miowak promised. She went to the shelf and took down a pair of boots. "You want boots like these."

Achebuk looked at them closely. "Yes, these good boots."

Ongan stood up. "Boots Miowak make never leak."

"Who they for?" Achebuk wanted to know.

"I make these for Nipchuk," Miowak replied putting them back.

"No see Nipchuk long time. He find gold?"

Ongan shook his head. Barney spoke up. "Uncle Charlie hasn't heard from him yet."

Ongan turned to Barney. "Where he look for gold?"

Barney thought a minute. "I think he said he was going near an old reindeer camp."

"Old reindeer camp near where I hunt seal," Achebuk said, "maybe same one."

But Barney had stopped listening. He was thinking maybe he and Anagik could help Nipchuk prospect when break-up came and he was a Sourdough.

All at once he realized Achebuk was saying something to him. Then he apologized. "I'm sorry, I didn't hear what you said."

"He say Ongan go seal hunting with him. You too," Miowak explained.

Barney sat up very straight. *Seal hunting with Achebuk, the best hunter in the village!*

"I'd sure like that!"

"Good." Achebuk walked to the door. "I go now." Then he stopped. "You be ready to hunt seal with Achebuk. You have gun?"

"Uncle Charlie gave me a rifle for Christmas."

"You have waterproof boots?"

Barney put out his foot. "Won't these do?" They were

the reindeer boots Uncle Charlie had given him.

Achebuk shook his head. "No good for hunting seal. Get too wet. You need boots like Miowak make for me."

"I make seal skin boots for Barney too," Miowak said in her soft voice.

Barney didnt know what to say. All in the same evening he was offered the chance to go seal hunting with the best hunter in the village and a new pair of boots. He wanted to pay Miowak but he didn't know how much to offer. Then he had an idea.

"I'll bring you the first seal I get," he promised her and everyone laughed.

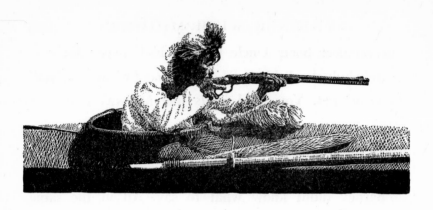

11

BARNEY GOES SEAL HUNTING

"We go to edge of ice field now," Achebuk announced, calling to his dog team to "gee."

Barney's heart skipped a beat. That meant three miles away from shore and the ice wasn't too strong, now that spring was here—Achebuk had said so. But out they went—the dogs splashing through pools of water. At the edge of the field, Barney could see the dark, cold Bering Sea before him. Big pieces of loose ice floated slowly past.

"Ice field breaking up," Achebuk said, pointing to one of the floes. As he watched, Barney could almost imagine the ice they were on rising and falling.

Achebuk slipped a white cloth parka over his fur parka. "Now, I white like ice cake. Seal no see me. We drive along here and look for them."

"Have you ever gone through the ice, Achebuk?" Barney asked.

"Naga (no)," the old hunter shook his head, "first time, last time with Eskimo."

"What do you mean first time, last time?"

"Eskimo can't swim. Water too cold all year to learn."

"You can't swim!" Barney exclaimed. "Aren't you afraid to be out on this ice?"

Achebuk shrugged his shoulders. "Eskimo no think of danger or he be no good hunting seal."

Their trail at the edge of the ice was rough. Here and there, snow had blown into big ridges and piles of ice blocked their way. When they came to these, Barney helped guide the kayak which was riding on a sled tied to the back of the dog sled.

"Hard trail," Achebuk said, "but better than by land."

Barney had to agree. All the snow had melted from the tundra even before school was out a week ago.

Just then Achebuk stopped the dogs and pointed out

to sea. It was a seal! Barney could just see its head bobbing through the water.

"He too far out," Achebuk whispered, "we try to bring him closer."

He took his ice pick and started scraping the point of it on the ice. After a few scratches, he stopped to see if the seal would come to see what the noise was. Barney held his breath. For just a second, it seemed the seal might turn back, but then it swam on out of sight.

"Too bad," Achebuk said, "but we have another chance. Seal hunting good this year. I already bring back twenty-two."

Achebuk was right. It wasn't long before he stopped the dogs again.

"Look!" he whispered excitedly and pointed straight ahead. "Big seal sleeping on edge of ice!"

Sure enough! Barney could see a black object lying close to the water not more than a hundred feet away.

"We on right side of wind, too," Achebuk added. "Seal no smell us."

"Won't he see us?" Barney whispered anxiously.

Achebuk didn't answer. He was busy slipping off his white cloth parka.

"You put on over fur parkee. Seal think you piece of ice."

"But aren't you going, too?"

Achebuk shook his head. "No. This your seal."

While Barney slipped into the white cloth parkee, Achebuk told him what to do.

"You crawl on hands and knees and belly like time I help you off river ice. If seal look up, hide face. Don't move. Don't make noise. Seal hear you he go in water."

Barney picked up his rifle with trembling fingers and started out. He was so afraid of being heard he hardly dared to breathe. Once when he was crawling between two cakes of ice, the seal raised its head and looked all around. Barney ducked his face and lay perfectly still for he didn't know how long, but when he rose to his knees again the seal had settled down. He could almost feel Achebuk watching him. Just like the time he'd crawled off the broken river ice. The closer he came, the bigger the seal looked.

At last Barney was near enough for a good shot. Suppose he should miss! He just couldn't. This was supposed to be Miowak's seal to pay for the fine new waterproof boots he was wearing.

Slowly he raised his rifle and braced his arm to shoot.

At that exact instant the seal raised its head, took a quick look around and before Barney could even fire one shot, slid over the few feet of ice and plopped into the sea.

Barney was stunned. He couldn't believe the seal was gone. He lowered his rifle. Well, I sure foozled that, he said to himself disgustedly. Then he heard a noise behind him. Achebuk was untying the kayak from its sled.

"I go after seal with harpoon," he called to Barney as he lowered the boat into the water and quickly slipped in. Achebuk paddled in a wide circle. Suddenly Barney saw the seal's head in the water, so did Achebuk. The old hunter swiftly went toward the seal, raised his harpoon and brought it down in one motion. There was a big splashing in the water. Achebuk had bagged a seal!

Barney held the dogs while Achebuk pulled the seal out of the water.

"Here your seal," Achebuk grinned proudly.

"No, he's yours," Barney corrected. "You're the one who killed him."

"All right," Achebuk agreed. "My seal."

He rewound the thong around his harpoon, lashed the kayak back to its sled and they started out again.

Barney trotted beside the sled with his rifle in hand. He wasn't taking any chances on missing another seal, but even though both Achebuk and he watched the edge of the ice constantly, they didn't see another seal for two hours.

They came to a section of ice flat as a table top.

"Thin ice," Achebuk said, "it form since last time I here. Maybe too thin." He turned the dogs over to Barney and putting on his snow shoes, walked ahead to test it with his ice pick as they went along.

When Barney drove the dogs on to the new ice, he noticed a crack running as far as he could see up and down the field.

"What about this crack, Achebuk?" He couldn't help but sound worried.

Achebuk turned around. "It all right as long as no wind blow from shore. Wind come up might blow this ice we on out to sea." He paused. "You afraid?"

"A little," Barney admitted.

Achebuk laughed. "Eskimo heart beat differently out on ice too." He looked out at the distant ice floes. "My be seal out there. I go in kayak and see."

Barney waved good luck to his friend, then sat down, rifle in hand to watch for seal himself. Suddenly he heard a noise. It was the dogs, all on their feet, tails high, ears cocked. Barney jumped up and ran to the sled. Just in time, he clamped his foot down on the brake and yelled whoa. The dogs had smelled another dog team. Barney could barely see it traveling far away on the ice. While he watched, the driver stopped his dogs and started over toward Barney. As the man came closer, Barney could see who it was.

"Why, hello, Nipchuk," Barney yelled in greeting. He remembered the first time he'd seen Nipchuk—when the old Eskimo had brought in a duck with gold in its gizzard. Then he remembered the last time he'd helped Nipchuk get together a grubstake to go out and prospect for gold for Uncle Charlie. Maybe Nipchuk had found gold!

"Hello, young friend!" Nipchuk rushed up to Barney and grabbed his hand. "You first person I see in long time. What you do here?"

Barney told Nipchuk he was hunting with Achebuk and, even though he didn't like to, he described how he'd missed the seal.

"But what are you doing here, Nipchuk? I thought you were prospecting. Did you find any gold?"

"I through prospecting," the old Eskimo shook his

head sadly, "I no find gold. Not ever' prospector find gold." Then he added slyly, "Not ever' seal hunter get seal." They both laughed at the joke.

Barney invited Nipchuk to stop and camp with him and Achebuk, but Nipchuk shook his head.

"I go home. Break-up come soon. I get home before ice go out."

As Barney waved good-bye he thought of Nipchuk's words—"Break-up come soon." Break-up! Barney could hardly wait. When that happened he would be a real Alaskan Sourdough. Then he and Anagik could go prospecting at last.

All at once, Barney shivered. The air was getting cold. Dark clouds covered the sun. A sharp wind was blowing. Barney looked out toward sea for Achebuk. The water was choppy. There was no sign of his friend. Just then Barney remembered Achebuk's words—"It all right as long as no wind blow from shore."

He turned toward land. The wind smacked his face. It was from the shore! The ice might break loose and start out to sea at any moment. Where could Achebuk be? Barney looked anxiously among the distant floes. No Achebuk! Had his kayak turned over in the rough water?

Barney began to walk up and down. What should he do? Should he try to get the dogs ashore or should he wait for Achebuk? The dogs who'd been lying down were on their feet. They knew something was wrong too. Barney looked out to sea again. Still no Achebuk, but then—something dark showed around the corner of an ice floe. It was the nose of the kayak! Achebuk was coming in! His light kayak tossed around like an egg shell. Barney stood and watched. He could see Achebuk's face, set and serious. Achebuk paddled a little way up from where Barney was waiting and slid in between an ice floe and the ice field where the water was a little calmer. As soon as he was within reach, he sunk his ice pick into the ice and drew his kayak closer. Barney helped him pull the light skin boat out of the water and tie it to the kayak sled. The minute this was fastened to the dog sled, Achebuk called to the dogs to go. Barney took a running jump on to the sled and they raced toward the place they'd first crossed onto smooth ice.

In a few seconds, Barney began to see a dark line before them. The line widened as they came closer. It was water! *Open Water! Twenty-five feet* separating the ice fields. They could not cross and the ice they were on was going out to sea!

Achebuk didn't waste any time. He steered the dogs to the left, by the open water.

"Maybe water get narrow farther on," he said.

Barney could see Achebuk was worried. His mouth was in a straight, grim line. They rode on for several minutes. The dogs raced along without any urging. Barney never took his eyes off of that channel of dark cold water separating them from safety. It did not narrow. If anything, it seemed to be growing wider. Finally Achebuk stopped the dogs. Barney looked at him.

"What are we going to do?"

Achebuk took a long look at the channel of water. "We cross here," he said calmly.

Barney looked at the water and then back at Achebuk. Had he heard right? Cross that twenty-five feet of water! How? But Achebuk didn't take time to explain.

"You unload sled," he ordered as he tied one end of a long rope to his leader's collar. Then quickly, he unlaced the kayak, pushed it into the water and paddled across. Once on the other side, he started pulling the rope and calling to his leader. When the dogs balked, Achebuk yelled, "Push 'em in, Barney, push 'em in."

By now, Barney had the sled emptied. He ran to the leader and shoved him in. The dog yelped as he hit the ice cold water but he swam toward Achebuk who guided him with the rope. Barney pushed the rest of the team in, then the empty sled. It made quite a parade across the dark stretch of water. Barney watched, feeling very sorry for the dogs. But that's better than their being lost at sea he told himself.

Once across Achebuk helped the soaked and shivering dogs onto the ice, then pulled the sled up.

Barney began to wonder how he was going to get across. He was relieved to see Achebuk climb into his kayak and start back, but there was more to be done before Barney could cross. First the dried fish for the dogs, camping equipment, guns, food and stove had to be packed in and on top of the kayak and taken across.

It took Achebuk three trips, then he came back the fourth time for Barney. He jumped out on the ice and pointing to the kayak ordered Barney to get in.

"Me paddle your kayak!" Barney knew the light boats turned over very easily.

"Naga (no), I paddle. You crawl inside. Lie down."

Barney did as he was told. The inside of the skin boat was dark, cold and damp but it would carry

Barney to safety. He felt a rolling motion. They were crossing. Barney was having a kayak ride in the Bering Sea but not exactly as he wished!

At last there was a soft thud. Achebuk had reached the other side. He pulled himself out. Then Barney crawled through the round opening on to safe, shore-bound ice. He and Achebuk looked at each other and grinned. Barney took the first deep breath he'd had since the wind started blowing. Finally Achebuk spoke.

"We start home now. Maybe travel all night. Storm weaken ice all along coast. Break-up getting close."

Break-up getting close! If both Nipchuk and Achebuk had said it, then it must be true.

"How long do you suppose it will be until break-up comes, Achebuk?" Barney asked trotting beside the sled to rest the dogs.

"No way to tell day, but soon," the old hunter answered.

Barney wasn't satisfied. He wanted to know the exact day he would become a Sourdough. If it would be soon, he and Anagik had to start making plans for prospecting. Everything would have to be discussed with Uncle Charlie. All of their equipment would have to be collected. Where would be the best place to set up camp, how long would it take to get there? How long would they stay? Where would they look for gold? *Would they really find anything?*

A hundred questions crowded into Barney's mind on the trip back to Unalakleet. By the time they reached the Trading Post, it was almost ten o'clock but Barney wasn't tired at all. He thanked Achebuk for taking him on such a thrilling seal hunt, then grabbing his gear raced upstairs.

"Uncle Charlie, Uncle Charlie, where are you?"

"Here I am, Barney." Uncle Charlie walked in from the back storage room. "How was the hunt?"

Barney realized he'd almost forgotten the hunt, he was so excited about break-up coming.

"Oh, I almost shot a seal but he went into the water, then Achebuk harpooned him; but, Uncle Charlie, I saw Nipchuk while we were down the coast and he says break-up is getting near. Achebuk says so too. When do you think it will happen?"

"Well, now there's no way of telling exactly. More and more sea ice is going out every night and the river mouth is open but parts of the river ice seem pretty solid yet. It might be a couple of days—it might be a week. "Now"—Uncle Charlie added with a smile—"if that answers your question, you might set down your sleeping bag and take off your parka."

Barney grinned. He'd completely forgotten he was still holding his camp gear. As Uncle Charlie had said, gold certainly did make one forget everything! And it *had* been gold he was thinking of, and of when he could go prospecting.

"Well, do you think—" Barney stopped in the middle of another question. He'd heard the whir of a ptarmigan! He hurried to open the front door.

"Come in, Anagik. I just got back. Look's like I'm going to be a Sourdough pretty soon and we can go prospecting. Nipchuk and Achebuk and Uncle Charlie think break-up may come any time."

"Yes, that's why I came," Anagik sounded excited too. "I thought we ought to talk things over."

"I wish I could leave the Trading Post and go with you boys, but I'll just have to be satisfied to grubstake you," Uncle Charlie told them bringing in some paper and a pencil so Barney could write down the things they should take.

"I wish you could go too, Uncle Charlie."

"Maybe next time. Now let's get to work."

When it was finished, the list was a long one. They

would be gone at least two weeks and besides the food and tent, they would have to take shovels and gold pans.

"Looks like a lot of gear," Uncle Charlie said glancing over the paper.

Anagik looked worried. "I know. After break-up, your dogs will have to go over tundra, Barney. It'll certainly be a heavy load."

"Oh, they can do it. I know they can," Barney said positively.

"They probably could," Uncle Charlie agreed. "Still I think it would be better if I had Tagiak take you up river by boat when the river's clear of ice."

Barney hated to admit it, but Uncle Charlie and Anagik were right. Dog sledding over dry tundra would be hard work for the dogs and for their driver. Still, he was sorry to think his dog-team driving days were over.

Anagik seemed to know what he was thinking.

"I tell you what let's do, Barney. Let's take the dogs out on one last run tomorrow. We'll go up river and I'll show you the place we'll go prospecting."

"Now that's a fine idea," Uncle Charlie approved.

"That'll be great, Anagik. What time can we leave?"

"Early," his friend answered, "this will probably be

our last run with the dogs for this year so we'll make it a good one."

Barney felt happy again. Soon break-up would come, soon he would be a real Alaskan Sourdough, but before that there would be one more trip with Seegoo!

12

LAST TRIP WITH SEEGOO

Anagik let out a yell and jumped from Barney's sled shaking the water off his parka.

"You sure soaked me that time," he laughed coming up to where Barney had stopped Seegoo and the team.

"I'm sorry, Anagik," Barney apologized, "I didn't realize that puddle was so deep."

The river ice was covered with pools of water and split by narrow open channels. The sound of running water could be heard everywhere.

"Well, come on, Barney," Anagik took his place in the sled again, "we'd better get started if we're going to get up river and back today."

"Do we have to go much farther?" Barney asked giving Seegoo the starting signal.

"Not much. Just around the next bend."

Barney dodged around a big puddle.

"What makes you think that will be a good place to prospect?"

"Well, it's marshy and a lot of birds and ducks feed there. Maybe, the duck Nipchuk brought you had eaten there." Anagik pointed to three cottonwood trees growing out of one trunk. "That's the place we cut off. The marsh is just over the hill."

Anagik helped Barney push the loaded sled over the river bank and part way up the hill. There was no snow at all and the going much harder. The sun was so warm, they soon took off their parkas. The dogs were panting, their tongues hanging out. Anagik stopped and brushed his arm across his forehead. "Just a little farther now."

"Whew!" Barney sank to the ground. "I guess it's a good thing we're not going prospecting by dog team."

"It would be slow traveling! I tell you what—let's stake the dogs out and walk the rest of the way."

Barney gladly agreed. They quickly chained the dogs, then set out for the marsh.

As Barney stepped over a log, he heard a familiar whirring noise. It was the ptarmigan call he and Anagik used to signal each other. He turned to find out what his friend wanted, but before he quite knew what was happening, there was a shot. Anagik ran over and held up a bird a little larger than a pigeon with brown and white feathers.

"It's a ptarmigan."

"I know, but I thought at first that whistle came from you. You sound more like a ptarmigan than a real ptarmigan does!"

"It's almost brown now," Anagik pointed out. "In winter, they're white and hard to see against the snow."

They started climbing again. At the top of the hill Anagik stopped and waved his arm. "That's where the gold is—maybe."

"There?" Barney looked ahead. It was just like a lot of other marshes, still he couldn't help but be especially interested in this one. "Let's go down for a closer look."

"I wish we could, but the water's too high yet. After break-up it'll go down. See where all those reeds are?" Anagik pointed in the center of the marsh. "That's a sand bar. We'll look there first."

Barney took a good look and shivered with excitement. Perhaps he was looking at the very spot he and Anagik would strike gold!

While Barney daydreamed, Anagik was busy picking some green shoots growing beside a creek.

"What are they for?" Barney asked.

"To eat," his friend replied. "We'll have them for lunch. I brought some seal oil. They're good with that."

And they really were!

Later, when Barney was sitting by the fire eating, he decided the greens made a very fine salad with his ptarmigan drumsticks.

"Boy!" he said, scraping a last bite of meat off the bone, "this is mighty fine eating. I hope you'll get all the meals when we're prospecting."

"We live good up here," Anagik replied. "Soon after break-up, we put in our vegetable gardens. Then the herring and salmon runs start."

"Gee, I wish I'd be here for that!" Barney exclaimed.

"When will you be leaving?" Anagik tried to sound casual but didn't succeed very well.

Barney waited a minute to answer because he didn't like to think of leaving Anagik and all his new friends, yet he was getting anxious to see his family and friends in Porterville.

"I leave on the first plane after we come back from prospecting," he answered finally.

"I'll be sorry to see you go."

Barney looked up.

"I wish you could come and visit me in the States sometime."

"Maybe I can," Anagik said. "I'm trying to earn enough money to go to High School somewhere—"

"Gee, that would be great! You could live with me. I don't have any brothers—just one sister—"

"Yes, you told me you had a sister, Barney. How old is she?" Anagik asked.

"Oh, she's just a little girl," Barney smiled. "She made me promise to bring her a fur parka and boots for her doll when I came back. Miowak's making some for her now."

"What are you going to do with Seegoo?"

"Why, I'll take him back on the plane with me." Barney went over to his leader. "I couldn't leave you, old boy, could I? Not after you saved my life in the blizzard last winter."

Anagik put down his plate "shhhh!"

Then he sat straight up—listening.

"Do you hear anything strange?"

At first Barney wasn't sure he did hear a noise. Then slowly he realized there was a rumbling sound—almost like distant thunder.

"Come on!" Anagik began running. "Lets get down to the river quick. I think break-up's starting."

Break-up! So soon?

Barney ran after his friend. As they came close to the river, the rumbling grew louder. There were sharp cracking sounds and in between muffled pounding.

Anagik stood on the bank and looked up river.

"Yep, it's break-up all right—up river about a half mile. See that wall of ice?"

Barney looked in the direction Anagik was pointing and whistled in amazement. There was a high grinding mass of ice stretching from bank to bank. It was like a dam holding back the open water of the river behind it. As it ground forward, the river ice in front split and buckled into the air.

Break-up! So it was coming at last. And now I'll be a Sourdough, Barney thought to himself. And what a show I'm seeing, too!

Anagik turned to Barney. "We'd better go back on

the hill to watch. This may be flooded. The dogs are far enough away so the water won't reach them."

"Anagik," Barney caught at the other boy's sleeve. "How in the world are we going to get back to the village?"

"Just like we did that last quarter of a mile to camp —overland—and it'll be just as hard."

"Uh-oh," Barney groaned, thinking of pushing the sled over bare tundra all the way back.

They trotted up the hill. As the ice ground and crunched forward, the muddy river streamed over the bank where, just a few moments before, Barney and Anagik had been standing. The water began to run more swiftly. Faster and faster it went by, now in a roar. Trees and stumps and chunks of ice churned together in the raging waters. It was a thrilling and noisy sight. They watched it until the last piece of brush and ice had disappeared downstream.

Anagik turned to Barney. "Congratulations! You're an Alaskan Sourdough now."

Barney grinned. Then he solemnly shook hands with Anagik, trying not to show how proud he was. He had done it! He had lived through an Alaskan winter, had seen the freeze-up and the break-up! He was a real

Alaskan Sourdough and now he could go prospecting.

The water was flowing more slowly and the flood water had gone down enough for them to stand on the river bank but not in the spot where they'd first watched the break-up. That section of the bank had been torn away by the grinding ice, leaving only rock and gravel on the sandy beach.

It made a nice place for Barney to wash the lunch dishes. As he swished their tin plates around in the water, he thought over the day's happenings.

There had been so much excitement with the break-up and his becoming a Sourdough, they hadn't started back as soon as they'd planned. Now with the ice gone, it would be late in the evening before they would get back to Unalakleet. "Then," Barney told himself, scooping up some sand to clean out the skillet, "we'll come back and prospect just as soon as we can get ready."

But Barney never finished cleaning the skillet. His hand stopped in mid-air, as he stared and stared at the sand.

"Anagik!" he finally yelled, dropping everything but the handful of sand and running to their camp.

"What?" Anagik came toward him. "What is it?"

Barney opened his hand.

"Look! Look what I've found. It's gold in the sand. Gold nuggets! Like those in the duck gizzard!" Barney was shaking so Anagik had to hold his hand steady to see.

"You're right! You're right! Barney. It is gold. Where'd you find it?"

"Down where the river washed the bank away during break-up."

"Come on," Anagik started out full speed. "Let's go!"

They raced down to where Barney had left their luncheon dishes and knelt beside the water. Anagik scooped up a tin plate full of sand and water, then with the round rolling motion Slim had shown Barney, spilled the water and sand out and there in the bottom of the pan was more gold!—nuggets—and one of them was almost as large as a pea. Barney did just as Anagik had done and ended up with a sprinkling of gold flakes and tiny nuggets, too.

Anagik sank back on his heels. "Barney, you've hit it! You've discovered gold!"

"Oh, Anagik, how much do you suppose there is? Do you really think it'll be worth anything?"

"I don't know. These nuggets are sort of big."

"Yes, but Slim Dixon once had $3,000 in a clean-up and then it just turned out to be a pocket."

"Well, you'll have to work it and see. Anyway, you've made a strike!"

"It's *our* strike, Anagik." Barney had a hard time keeping his voice calm. "Remember, before we started out, we said fifty-fifty. What do we do now?"

"We get back to the village just as soon as we can to have your Uncle Charlie file a claim on this land for us," Anagik answered picking up the pans and dishes. "After that we'll come back and set up our sluice box, *then* we'll know if we've hit pay dirt or not."

"Good!" Barney agreed.

They hurried back to camp. While Anagik put out the fire, Barney hitched Seegoo and the team.

"Ready?" Barney looked up.

"You bet!" Anagik came back to help Barney push. The empty sled grated and scraped over the bare ground.

As the afternoon wore on and the sun grew warmer, they had to stop more often to rest the dogs and themselves. Then Barney would forget all about his sore back and feet for they would talk about their gold discovery.

Anagik said he would spend some of his to come outside and go to high school. Barney could think of a hundred things he would buy for his family.

Once back in the village Barney and Anagik suddenly forgot their aching legs and ran up the stairs of the Trading Post two at a time.

"Uncle Charlie," Barney yelled, "Uncle Charlie, are you home?"

"I sure am," the big man appeared at the head of the stairs. "Is something wrong?"

Barney bounded into the kitchen and took the gold he and Anagik had panned out of his handkerchief.

"Look!"

"Great Christopher!" Uncle Charlie exclaimed blinking his eyes. "Gold! Where'd you find that?"

"Anagik knows the place. We want you to file a claim for us so we can mine it."

"You bet I will. Nothing I'd like to do better." Uncle Charlie walked over to his desk and motioned for Barney and Anagik to sit down. "Now let's hear all about it."

Barney began the story. Anagik took it up where they had started panning. Then Barney broke in again.

"Oh, Uncle Charlie, how much do you suppose our

discovery will be worth? Will we make any money at all?"

"Well, it's hard to tell at this stage," Uncle Charlie said thoughtfully. "Still, with colors like this in your pan, you've either come upon a gold pocket lying on the bed rock or you *might* have discovered a real rich section of mining land. In either case you'll have a good amount of money coming." Now Uncle Charlie's voice was full of excitement, too. "Where did you say you found this gold?"

"Right at the spot we'd been standing watching break-up," Barney answered.

Uncle Charlie slapped the table with his hand.

"I'd almost forgotten, Barney. Congratulations! You're a real Alaskan Sourdough, only you did better than most of them. *You found gold!*"

Barney couldn't think of a thing to say. So many exciting things had happened all at once.

"Also in case you're interested," Uncle Charlie went on, "you became a Sourdough on May 16th at twenty minutes after one."

Barney grinned. "I'm glad you noticed what time it was. I'll want to write home about that."

"You'll have something else to write home, too, Barney," Anagik broke in. "Our gold discovery."

"*Will* I? You bet I will. That'll be a story—our last sled trip and what happened!"

"And Barney," it was Uncle Charlie, "don't forget to tell them it all started in the gizzard of a duck!"